Boy-Crazy Stacey

Look for these and other books in the Baby-sitters Club series:

#1 *Kristy's Great Idea*
#2 *Claudia and the Phantom Phone Calls*
#3 *The Truth About Stacey*
#4 *Mary Anne Saves the Day*
#5 *Dawn and the Impossible Three*
#6 *Kristy's Big Day*
#7 *Claudia and Mean Janine*
#8 *Boy-Crazy Stacey*
#9 *The Ghost at Dawn's House*

Boy-Crazy Stacey

Ann M. Martin

SCHOLASTIC INC.
New York Toronto London Auckland Sydney

This book is for
June and Ward Cleaver
(alias Noël and Steve)
from the Beav

ISBN 0-590-41040-7

12 11 10 9 8 7 6 5 4 3 2 7 8 9/8 0 1 2/9

Printed in the U.S.A. 11

First Scholastic printing, November 1987

"Mom?" I said. "How do you think you're supposed to behave in a mansion?"

My mother looked up from the letter she was writing at the desk in our den. "What, Stace?" she asked.

"This is the evening we're all going over to Watson's. I mean, to Kristy's. And I want to make sure I do everything right."

"You've been to Mr. Brewer's house before, honey," replied Mom.

"I know, but not just for a regular visit. Kristy says all her neighbors are really fancy. Remember how we had to fix up Louie the day before the Thomases moved, just so he would look as nice as all the other dogs in the new neighborhood?"

My mother smiled. "Sometimes Kristy gets carried away. You know that. I think you should just go over there and behave the same way you would have in Kristy's old house."

"Really?"

"Really. When are you supposed to be there, honey?"

"In about an hour. Mr. Kishi's driving Claudia and Mary Anne and me over as soon as he gets home from work."

"And will you be — "

"Yes, Mom. I'll be careful about what I eat."

"Stacey, there's no need to be rude."

"But you know I'm always careful. And Kristy is really nice about making sure there's plain popcorn or fruit or something for me. Besides, this is just a *little* party. Just supper. And then I'll be home."

The members of the Baby-sitters Club were all going over to the new home of Kristy Thomas, our club president. She and her mother and brothers had moved there not long ago when her mother got remarried to Watson Brewer, this really nice guy who also happens to be a really rich guy. He lives in a neighborhood where the yards are big enough for swimming pools or tennis courts, and all the houses are set way back from the road. Some of them are hidden by walls or bushes.

Until she moved, though, Kristy had lived in a regular old house on regular old Bradford Court, next door to her best friend, Mary Anne Spier, who's our club secretary, and across the street from Claudia Kishi, our vice-president and *my* best friend. It was Kristy's idea to start a business doing baby-sitting for the families in our neighborhood, and it worked out really well. The four of us, plus Dawn Schafer, who lives not far away, meet for about a half an hour three afternoons a week in Claudia's bedroom. Our clients phone us looking for baby-sitters and they almost always get one, since they reach five sitters (I should say, five *qualified* sitters) at once.

We have a record book with all sorts of information, including our schedules, and Mary Anne keeps track of our jobs and who's available to sit when, and things like that. Kristy insists that we also keep the Baby-sitters Club Notebook, in which each of us has to write up every single sitting job we do. Then the book gets passed around so the others can read about what happened. It's pretty useful.

This summer, our club branched out a little. Last month, July, we did our regular baby-sitting *and* held a play group. We held it right here in my backyard. The neighborhood kids came over three mornings a week for games and stories and art projects. It worked out really well.

But July was over. It was the beginning of August. And for the first time since the club began almost a year ago, at the beginning of seventh grade, we baby-sitters were going to be scattered, split up. Before that happened, Kristy wanted to have a get-together. And she wanted to have it at her new house. That was fine with the rest of us. We love Watson's house, even though it makes us a little nervous sometimes.

I went to my bedroom and began looking through my closet. Why hadn't I done this earlier? I realized I would have to choose my outfit very carefully. I wanted to be casual enough to have fun, but sophisticated enough to look impressive in case any rich neighbors dropped by. I also wanted to be cool since it felt like it was about 150 degrees outside. I changed my mind six times before I decided on this new pink shirt I got the last time we went back to New York City to visit friends. Big, bright green and yellow birds were splashed all over it. It was gigantic, so it would be cool. I put it on with a pair of baggy shorts, looped a wide green belt around my middle, and hunted up some jewelry — silver bangle bracelets and a pair of silver earrings shaped like bells that actually ring when they dangle back and forth.

I'm working on making Mom and Dad let me get my ears pierced a second time so I can wear two pairs of earrings at once, but so far, no luck. I pretty much grew up in New York — we just moved here to Stoneybrook, Connecticut, a year ago — and I have sort of wild taste. My parents have let me get away with a lot of things fashionwise, but they draw the line at two earrings in each ear. They said I would look like a pirate, although I, personally, have never seen a pirate with more than exactly one earring. I pointed out that if I *did* get my ears pierced again, probably no one would mistake me for a pirate, but Mom and Dad failed to see the humor in that.

Beep! Beep!

I heard honking and looked out my window. The Kishis' car was in my driveway. Mr. Kishi was at the wheel; Mimi, Claudia's grandmother, was next to him; and Claudia was in the backseat with Mary Anne Spier.

"I'll be right there!" I shouted.

I thundered down the stairs. "'Bye, Mom!"

"Wait, Stacey," she said, coming into the front hall.

"Mom, I have to go!"

My mother thrust a small, foil-wrapped package into my hand. "Here. Take this with you."

"What is it?"

"Apple slices."

"Mom, I promise you there will be stuff I can eat at Watson's. He's got the biggest kitchen I've ever seen. I'm sure, somewhere, there's an apple." I handed the package back to her. "Put them in the fridge, okay? I'll eat them tomorrow."

My parents worry about me constantly because I've got diabetes. That means I have to be very careful to eat a certain amount of sugar every day — not too much and not too little. If I'm not careful, my blood sugar level goes all kerflooey and I can get really sick. My parents are always afraid I'll sneak off and eat junk food. I've been tempted, but I've never done it. Why would I want to get sick?

I dashed out the front door. "See you!" I called to Mom.

My father was gardening in one of the flower beds. It's his favorite early evening activity in the summer.

"'Bye, Dad!" I called.

"'Bye, honey. Be careful."

Be careful. I should have known. But I reminded myself that they're a lot better than they used to be. Just a little over a year earlier, my parents practically wouldn't let me go to school.

I scrambled into the backseat of the Kishis' car. "Hi, everybody! Hi, Mimi!"

Mimi eased herself around and smiled. "Hello, Stacey," she answered slowly. (Mimi had a stroke this summer and she's still recovering. She moves awkwardly and has some trouble speaking.)

I could tell that Claudia and Mary Anne were as excited as I was about going to Kristy's. The three of us were wriggling around like puppies. But we quieted down when we reached Kristy's new neighborhood. And by the time Mr. Kishi had pulled into the circular drive and Watson's house had loomed into view, we were positively silent.

I think it was the sight of Kristy that brought us back to reality. She was sprawled outside the elegant front door of Watson's house, eating a Popsicle, reading *People* magazine, and wearing cutoff jeans and a holey white T-shirt that said I ♡ MY followed by a silhouette of a collie. Her feet were bare.

The sight was refreshing. I knew then that my mother was right. No matter what Kristy's house looked like, Kristy was still Kristy. I wouldn't have to behave any differently.

Dawn arrived just as the back fender of Mr. Kishi's car was disappearing at the other end of the drive.

"Hi!" she cried, leaping out. "See you later, Mom!"

The five of us faced each other eagerly.

"Well, come on!" said Kristy.

We entered the front hall of her house and greeted her mother and Watson in the living room. Then we raced upstairs and down a hallway to the room Kristy had chosen for her bedroom. Watson's house is so big that Kristy and her three brothers each got a room of their own when they moved in. And even so, Watson's two little children from his first marriage, Karen and Andrew, who don't even live with him full-time, have their own rooms for when they visit, plus a playroom, and there are still a few guest rooms left over. It makes me sort of breathless. I mean, when I lived in New York, we had what was considered a pretty big apartment, and it only had four bedrooms, one of which was hardly big enough for a bed.

In Kristy's room, we all plopped down on the new comforter on her new bed, arranging ourselves around Louie, her collie, who was sprawled on his back.

"Where are your brothers?" I asked.

"David Michael's around somewhere," replied Kristy. (David Michael is seven.) "And Sam and Charlie are over at a neighbor's house using the pool." (Sam and Charlie are older, in high school.)

"Are sandwiches okay for dinner?" Kristy asked us. "Mom and I made a whole stack of them this afternoon. There are a couple of plain tuna fish for you, Stace."

"Great," I said. "Thanks."

I glanced at Mary Anne Spier. As I mentioned earlier, Mary Anne is Kristy's best friend, and Claudia is mine, but it's funny the way things work out. Mary Anne and *I* were going to be spending the next two weeks together. I was a little nervous about it. We are *so* different. Mary Anne is really shy; I'm pretty straightforward. Mary Anne is kind of young; I'm sophisticated. Mary Anne has no interest in boys; I had a couple of boyfriends in seventh grade.

As if reading my mind, Claudia said to me, "Are you all ready for the Pikes, Stace?"

"I hope so," I replied. "I've never spent two weeks with eight kids before. At least I'll have Mary Anne to help me."

"You guys are so lucky," said Kristy wistfully. "Two weeks at the beach."

"Two weeks of chasing after Claire, Margo, Nicky, Vanessa, Byron, Jordan, Adam, and Mallory," I pointed out.

"Well, I'd go to the beach in a second, even if I had to be a mother's helper," said Kristy.

As uncertain as I was about going off with

Mary Anne, I had to admit I was excited. The members of our club baby-sit for the Pikes often, and not long ago, Mrs. Pike had called to say she wanted two of us to go along with them as mother's helpers when they take their summer vacation down in Sea City, New Jersey. Mary Anne and I were the only ones available.

It was all part of why the Baby-sitters Club was going to scatter. In just a couple of days, Mary Anne and I would be off to Sea City, Claudia and her family were going on a quiet vacation to a mountain resort in New Hampshire, and Dawn and her younger brother were flying to California to visit their father. They hadn't been in California in seven months, since their parents got divorced and Mrs. Schafer decided to move back to Connecticut, where she grew up.

"I can't believe I'm stuck here in Stoneybrook while you guys get to go to all these great places," wailed Kristy.

"It *is* sort of ironic," spoke up Dawn. "I mean, here you are in this mansion with a rich stepfather. . . ."

"I know," said Kristy, looking a little pouty. "But Mom is determined to make our 'new' family work out. She wants us all together for a while."

Kristy's mom appeared at the door just then, carrying a big tray loaded with sodas and the sandwiches. As soon as she left, we dived into the food as if we hadn't eaten since July. When we were finished, we fooled around with new hair styles, and I tried on some of Kristy's clip-on earrings to see how I'd look if my parents were to go crazy or something and let me pierce my ears again after all.

"Uh-oh," said Dawn suddenly, looking at her watch. "It's almost nine. My mom said she'd pick me up between nine and nine-thirty."

"My dad's coming soon, too," said Claudia.

"I won't see you guys for over *two weeks!*" cried Kristy.

"Hey," said Mary Anne, "I've got an idea. Let's exchange our vacation addresses. Then we can all write postcards to each other."

Kristy found some index cards in her desk drawer and we wrote down our addresses for each other.

"I've got an even better idea," Kristy said. "Stacey and Mary Anne, why don't you write me a postcard every day describing your job with the Pikes? Later, we'll enter them in the notebook. That way, we'll keep it up-to-date and official."

"I might baby-sit for my old clients when I

go back to California," said Dawn. "If I do, I'll send you notebook entries, too."

We talked and made plans busily. We could hardly believe it when David Michael called, "Mr. Kishi and Mrs. Schafer are here!"

We baby-sitters looked at each other. Kristy began to cry. Then Dawn. Then Mary Anne. Then Claudia and me.

"I'm going to miss you!" wailed Dawn.

"I'm going to miss you and be bored!" added Kristy.

"I've never been away from home alone before!" cried Mary Anne.

We all began hugging each other. Kristy handed out tissues. As soon as we'd calmed down, Dawn moaned, "Two whole *weeks*," and the hugging and crying started again.

A few minutes later, Claudia, Mary Anne, and I climbed into the backseat of the Kishis' car. We sniffled all the way to Bradford Court.

I was miserable . . . until I got to my room and looked at my new bikini and began thinking of sunshine and the ocean and cute boys in bathing trunks and the boardwalk the Pike kids were always talking about. A little flutter of excitement crept into my stomach and pushed away the stone of misery. By the time I went to bed, I was so excited about Sea City, New Jersey, that I couldn't sleep.

There is nothing like ringing the doorbell at the Pikes' house. If the kids are at home, there is an actual stampede to get to the door.

Mary Anne and I stood on their front stoop the next afternoon. "Brace yourself," I said.

I rang the bell.

Pitter-patter, pitter-patter. Feet were running toward us.

Thump, thump, thump, thump. Thud, thud, thud, thud.

Crash.

The inner door was flung open. There stood Claire, Margo, Nicky, Vanessa, and Jordan. They looked flushed and breathless.

"Hi!" squealed Claire. Claire is the youngest Pike. She just turned five. Margo just turned seven, Nicky is eight, and Vanessa is nine. Jordan is ten, but he's not an ordinary ten-year-old — he's a triplet. Byron and Adam are his identical brothers. The oldest Pike is Mallory, who's eleven. She's a really good kid and usually gives us baby-sitters a hand. She even helped out at our play group last month.

I opened the screen door, and Claire grabbed my hand. "Come inside," she said urgently, tugging at me.

Not to be outdone, Margo grabbed Mary Anne's hand. "Yeah, come on in."

Vanessa, who is usually quiet, began jumping up and down. "Tomorrow, tomorrow, we go to Sea City!" she cried. "We'll see the beach and the shells so pretty."

Nicky rolled his eyes. "Do you have to rhyme *every*thing?" he asked.

"Yes," replied Vanessa. "Because I'm going to be a poet."

"You didn't rhyme *that,*" Nicky pointed out maddeningly, and Vanessa stuck out her tongue at him.

"Mo-om!" yelled Nicky. "Vanessa stuck her tongue out at me!"

We were standing in the narrow front hallway. Mary Anne and I were pinned against a closet door.

"Okay, kids," called Mrs. Pike, as she ran in from the kitchen. "Give Mary Anne and Stacey some breathing room."

The Pikes backed off.

Mrs. Pike had invited us over that afternoon

to discuss the trip and to explain our responsibilities. She ushered us into the living room and shooed the children outdoors. Then she began talking.

"Mostly," she said after a while, "you'll just be giving Mr. Pike and me a hand since, of course, we'll be there, too. But we would like some time to ourselves. So there will be afternoons or evenings when we'll go off to do things on our own. Then you'll be in charge."

Mary Anne and I nodded. I was beginning to think that "mother's helper" was a pretty funny term, since Mary Anne and I were going to be helping Mr. Pike as much as Mrs. Pike. Maybe we should be called parents' helpers.

"Have you ever been to the Jersey Shore?" asked Mrs. Pike.

"Nope," said Mary Anne.

"Once," I replied.

"Well, Sea City is a medium-sized town. There's a lot to see and do and you'll be perfectly safe on your own. Just keep a careful eye on the children. There's traffic to watch for, but there's also the ocean."

Mary Anne and I nodded again.

"As you know, Mr. Pike and I don't believe in making rules for the children or forcing them to do things they don't want to do. But we do make one beach rule which we expect everyone to stick to: Absolutely no going in the ocean — not even wading — before nine A.M. or after five P.M. Between nine and five the lifeguards are on duty, unless it's raining. Then you can swim as much as you want as long as you stay in front of the lifeguard station. Is that clear?"

"Yes," we said.

"I don't mean to sound harsh. It's just that the ocean can be so dangerous. But believe me, there are plenty of other things to do in Sea City. There's Trampoline Land and miniature golf. There's the boardwalk with an amusement park. There's a movie theater and shops and so many places to eat you can smell Sea City before you see it!"

I giggled.

"It's a great place for kids," Mrs. Pike added. "We've been going there for nine years. I know you'll have a good time."

Mrs. Pike went on to tell us about the house they always rented, food shopping, dividing up chores, and stuff like that. Then I told her about my diet and about the injections of insulin I have to give myself every day. Although the Pike kids don't know I have diabetes, Mr. and Mrs. Pike do, and they wanted to be sure I'd feel comfortable on the trip, and that they had the right kind of foods on hand for me. It was very nice of them.

Mrs. Pike had had to do a lot of fast talking to convince my parents to let me go to Sea City. It would be the first time I'd been away from Mom and Dad longer than overnight since I'd gotten diabetes almost two years ago. They didn't even think about letting me go until they'd looked up a couple of doctors in Sea City and spoken to them over the phone.

Mary Anne and I left the Pikes' that afternoon practically crackling with excitement. We were to leave at eight o'clock the next morning. It was time to go home and pack.

"I already packed," Mary Anne confided. "I couldn't wait. I'm scared, but I'm really looking forward to this. It's my first time away from my father, my first trip to the beach — and my first bikini! Dad said I could get one as long as the bottom part was decent."

Mary Anne's father used to be really strict with her. He's still a little strict, but he's much better. It's because Mrs. Spier died a long time ago and he's raised Mary Anne by himself. He loosened up a lot, though, when Mary Anne finally began standing up to him.

When I got home, I went to my room, opened

my suitcase on my bed, and began carefully laying my clothes in it — last year's bikini, the new bikini, two bright sundresses, sandals, shorts, tops, a nightshirt. Then I snuck over to my bottom bureau drawer, removed a bottle labeled SUN-LITE, and buried it under my clothes. I was determined to come home with lightened hair. My hair is already blonde, but I wanted it Sun-Lite blonde. However, if Mom saw the bottle, I'd be dead.

I hid it just in time, because the next thing I knew I heard my mother's footsteps on the stairs.

"Honey?" Mom called.

"In my room," I replied. "I'm packing."

Mom came in and perched on the edge of my bed. She watched me toss things into the suitcase. "Do you have everything?" she asked.

"I think so. Mary Anne and I asked Mrs. Pike about clothes and stuff this afternoon. She said no one dresses up in Sea City. A sundress would be fine if we went out to dinner."

"Do you have something to do down there?"

"Something to *do?!* I've got eight kids to watch."

"I know, but I'm sure you'll have a little

time to yourself. Do you have a book or some needlepoint?"

I held up both — an Agatha Christie mystery, and this swan I'd been needlepointing for about five years.

Mom nodded. "What about stamps? Do you have stamps so you can write postcards?" She was looking more and more nervous.

"No. But I'm sure there's a post office in Sea City."

"I'll get you some stamps," Mom said suddenly. "Be right back." She dashed into her bedroom and I could hear her rummaging around in her desk. When she returned, she handed me a strip of postcard stamps.

"Thanks," I said. I tucked them into my purse.

Next Mom asked about toothpaste. But I knew what she really wanted to ask me. She wanted to know if I'd been responsible enough to get together everything I'd need for two weeks of insulin injections. Finally I gave in and showed her. I opened the special travel kit she'd bought for me.

"See?" I said. "Everything's there."

"What about — "

"The doctors' numbers are in my purse. Mrs. Pike wrote them down, too. And she knows all about my diet. We talked about it today."

"Oh, Stacey," said Mom suddenly. "I'm so worried. I'm going to worry for the next two weeks."

"You really don't have to," I told her. I sat next to her on the bed. "The Pikes have a phone, remember? You can call if you want. And Mrs. Pike would call you if anything *did* happen — not that it's going to," I added quickly. "And don't call a lot, okay? I don't want the Pike kids to think I'm a baby. Then they'd never listen to me."

Mom looked at me for the longest time. Finally she opened her arms. I leaned over and we hugged. Mom cried. I cried a little, too. It's awfully hard helping your parents grow up.

But it has to be done.

CHAPTER 3

Saturday afternoon

Dear Kristy,

Hi! We made it. The drive down here was wild, but we arrived unharmed. Do you like this postcard? Mary Anne and I found a drugstore with these really wild cards. Here are some things to put in the Baby-sitters Club Notebook: Sometimes the Pike kids get carsick. Claire is still in her silly stage. She calls her mother "Moozie" and her father "Daggles." That's all for now. More tomorrow! 'Bye!

Luv,
Stacey

The next morning, I discovered the meaning of the word *madhouse*.

Mary Anne and I arrived at the Pikes' early. My dad drove us over. If you think Mom and I had been tearful the day before, you should have seen Mary Anne and her father. It was like Niagara Falls — for both of them. I've hardly ever seen a man cry.

But Mary Anne's tears were dry by the time we reached the Pikes'. My father pulled up in front of the house. He started to help Mary Anne and me with our suitcases.

"Just drop us off, Dad," I said. "Okay? You don't need to come with us or anything."

Dad was understanding. He simply gave me a hug, waved to Mr. Pike, then turned around and drove off.

Mr. Pike was struggling with the luggage rack. Actually, with two luggage racks. So many of us were going to Sea City that we had to drive down there in both of the Pike station wagons.

While Mr. Pike tried to fit suitcases into the luggage racks, Mrs. Pike and Mallory kept carrying boxes and things out of the house and depositing them by the cars.

"Hi, Stacey! Hi, Mary Anne!" cried Margo.

Claire ran out of the house and joined her

sister. I'd never seen anybody so excited. She looked as if she'd just had about ten cups of coffee.

"Hi, hi, Stacey-silly-billy-goo-goo!" Claire screeched. "Hi, Mary Anne-silly-billy-goo-goo!" She was galloping around in circles.

I rolled my eyes at Mary Anne. Claire was going through this incredibly silly stage. It could drive you crazy.

Mr. Pike finally finished hefting all the suitcases onto the luggage racks and securing them with rope. He turned around. Seven cartons were at his feet. "What's all this?" he demanded.

"Bedding," replied Mrs. Pike.

"Toys," added Nicky.

Mr. Pike groaned.

Forty-five minutes later, everything was loaded into or on top of the cars, including the people. I was sitting in the backseat of the car Mr. Pike was driving. Next to me was Nicky. Between us was a carton. At our feet was a large thermos. Sprawled out in the very back were Claire and Margo. Mallory was sitting up front with her father.

"You guys comfortable back there?" I asked the girls.

"Yup," replied Margo. "We have everything we need."

"So I see," I said. "Coloring books."

"Crayons," added Claire.

"Pillows," Nicky pointed out, turning around.

"Crackers," I said. "Barf Bucket. . . . Barf Bucket? What on earth is that?" Between the girls was a red plastic sand pail. It was carefully labeled PIKE BARF BUCKET in big letters.

"In case we get carsick," said Claire.

"Be sure to drink a lot of grape soda this morning," said Nicky, grinning wickedly. "That'd look neat coming up. Purple puke."

Claire and Margo laughed hysterically.

I closed my eyes. I absolutely can't stand it when someone gets sick. When I opened them, I caught sight of Mr. Pike looking at me in the rearview mirror.

"Don't worry," he said. "We rarely have to use it. We've only had a few emergencies that I can remember."

I smiled with relief.

Everyone was settled in the two cars. Mr. and Mrs. Pike had rolled down their windows and were calling last-minute instructions to each other. Things like, "It's the Garden State Parkway, not the New Jersey Turnpike," and, "Ice-cream stop at Howard Johnson's," and, "Try to follow me, but if we get separated, remember the real estate agent in Sea City is Ellen Cooke."

At last we backed out of the driveway.

"Good-bye, house!" called Nicky.

"Good-bye, house-silly-billy-goo-goo!" called Claire.

"Good-bye, Stoneybrook. Sea City, here we come!" added Mallory.

"Hey, Daggles-silly-billy-goo-goo," Claire said to her father. "Guess what."

"What, sweetie?" replied Mr. Pike, trying to cross an intersection with a four-way stop.

"That's what!"

Mr. Pike made it through the intersection and noticed a rope from the luggage rack flapping against the windshield. He pulled to a stop and got out to fix it.

"Are we there already?" asked Claire.

"We're still on our own *street*, stupid," Nicky said in disgust.

"Don't call her stupid," said Mallory, without even turning around.

"Stacey-silly-billy-goo-goo?" asked Claire.

I hesitated, not wanting to fall into the trap Mr. Pike had fallen into. "What?" I said at last.

"How much longer?"

"Several hours," I replied as Mr. Pike got back in the car. "It's a long drive. Why don't you and Margo open your coloring books? You can each make a picture to give to your mom when we get to the beach."

The girls opened their books and began sorting through their crayons. Nicky took a horrible-looking green monster out of his pocket and started to play with it. In the front seat, Mallory was reading *The Secret Garden*. We pulled onto the highway.

Everything was peaceful for about half an hour — until Mrs. Pike edged forward and passed us in the next lane. For some reason, we all happened to look up as the car went by. So we all saw that Jordan was holding up a big piece of paper in the side window that read BARFMOBILE. Jordan was pointing his finger at us and grinning. Obviously, he meant *we* were the Barfmobile.

"Barfmobile!" yelped Nicky. He sounded highly insulted. "You guys have any paper back there?" he asked, turning to his little sisters.

"Sure," replied Margo. "Paper, scissors, crayons — "

"Give me a piece of paper, quick," said Nicky. "And a red crayon."

Margo handed them to him. Nicky rested the paper against the carton and began scribbling.

"What are you writing, Nicky-silly-billy-goo-goo?" asked Claire about twelve times.

Nicky held up his masterpiece.

The paper read VOMIT COMET.

"That'll show them," remarked Mallory.

"Hey, Dad," said Nicky, hanging his arms over the front seat. "Speed up."

"Why?" asked Mr. Pike.

"I want you to pass Mom."

"Sorry, Nick–o. The traffic is too thick. Maybe when it clears up a little."

"Okay." Nicky flopped back into his seat, pouting.

The little girls went back to their coloring. Mallory returned to *The Secret Garden.*

But Nicky kept peering out the window, trying to spot his mother's car. "Jingle bells," he sang softly, "Batman smells, Robin laid an egg." He turned to me. "Get it, Stacey? *Robin* laid an *egg?*"

"I get it."

"Jingle bells, Batman smells, Robin laid an egg. . . ."

"Nicky, I really hate that song," said Mallory.

"Okay. Jingle bells, Santa smells, Rudolph broke his — Hey! Here we go!"

The traffic was very heavy. The cars in Mrs. Pike's lane were edging along, but the ones in our lane were suddenly moving a bit faster. As we passed the other Pike car, three things happened at once. Nicky triumphantly held up his sign and was rewarded with dirty looks from the triplets. Claire called, "Hi, Moozie-silly-billy-goo-goo!" to her mother. And Margo grabbed for the Barf Bucket and whimpered, "I don't feel too good."

"Uh-oh," I said.

"Darn," said Nicky. "She didn't have any grape soda yet."

Poor Margo looked so miserable, I couldn't turn away from her, even though if I saw her throw up, I'd probably have to use the bucket myself. She turned a wicked shade of green, but nothing happened.

"She might feel better if she sat up front," suggested Mallory.

"If you're going to trade places, do it carefully," said Mr. Pike grimly.

"Oh, boy!" squealed Nicky. "The last time this happened, Margo puked while she was climbing over the seats."

"Swell," I muttered.

The girls managed to switch places. Mallory accidentally kicked Mr. Pike in the shoulder, but Margo's breakfast stayed down.

"Jingle bells, Santa sm — " began Nicky.

"Nicholas, if we hear that song one more time . . ." threatened Mr. Pike. He was trying to pass a Mack truck.

"Okay," said Nicky. "Jingle barf — "

"Nicholas!"

"It's not that song!" Nicky exclaimed. "It's a different one." But he kept quiet after that.

"How many more minutes?" asked Claire.

"About fifteen and we'll stop for ice cream," said her father.

What a relief! The ice-cream break was just what we needed. Mary Anne and the Pike kids (including Margo, who claimed to be starving) slurped up big Howard Johnson's ice-cream cones. Mr. and Mrs. Pike had coffee. And I managed to find a Popsicle that was made with fruit only — no sugar. It was great. It's nice not to be left out of *every* food treat.

We climbed back into the cars and began the rest of the trip to Sea City. After a while, the ground began to look sandier. The trees became scrubbier and shorter. And finally Mallory spotted a sign that said SEA CITY, EXIT 10 MILES.

"Oh, boy!" she whooped.

The rest of us cheered.

Soon we were driving off the exit ramp, Mrs. Pike behind us, and turning onto a causeway that crossed some marshy land. The air smelled of salt.

"Hey, there's the cow sign!" cried Nicky pointing.

I looked to the right and saw a billboard with a three-dimensional purple cow. It was an advertisement for cream.

"There's Crabs for Grabs!" said Mallory as we passed a restaurant.

"There's the suntan girl!" Margo dissolved into giggles as we passed another billboard, this one showing a puppy pulling at the bottom of a little girl's bathing suit, showing off her splendid tan line.

"Why did Mr. Stupid tiptoe past the medicine chest?" shrieked Claire. "Because he didn't want to wake up the sleeping pills!" she answered herself.

"Okay, settle down," I told her.

The Pikes fell into silence as we entered Sea City. They looked awed, and I could see why. Their senses were suddenly overloaded with great kid stuff: the smell of hotdogs and fried food and the sea air, the sounds of the waves and of kids shouting and laughing and calling to each other, but mostly the sights. We passed Trampoline Land and miniature golf and souvenir stands. We passed stores and restaurants and ice-cream parlors. And in the distance was a boardwalk with arcades and a Ferris wheel and a roller coaster and probably plenty of head-spinning rides. And beyond all *that* gleamed the ocean.

Saturday night

Dear Claudia,

Hi! We've been in Sea City for half a day now. You should have seen the kids today after we got here. We went exploring as soon as we were unpacked, and they were so excited! There's so much to do here!

After we looked around the town we took a walk on the beach. I saw the most gorgeous boy! He's a lifeguard, and he's the guy of my dreams! See ya!

Luv,
Stace

Mr. Pike cruised down a wide street in Sea City. (He called it the main drag.) There were palm trees in front of a lot of the stores, but they were all plastic! I guess Sea City wasn't really palm tree country. Anyway, after a while he turned down a side street and stopped in front of a little pink house surrounded by white gravel. A sign in the yard read ELLEN COOKE, REALTOR. Mr. Pike went inside. He returned a few minutes later with a ring of keys and a folder full of fliers and ads and even an uninflated souvenir beach ball. We drove off again.

"I claim the ball!" cried Nicky.

"No, me!" yelled Margo.

"No, me!" yelled Claire.

I grabbed the beach ball and sat on it. "Guess what," I said. "The beach ball is either everybody's or nobody's."

"Thank you, Stacey," said Mr. Pike.

"But it can't be everybody's," said Nicky.

"Then I guess it's nobody's," I replied.

"If it's nobody's, then I claim it!" Nicky retorted gleefully.

Luckily, just then we turned into a driveway.

"Here we are!" announced Mr. Pike. "End of the line! Everybody out."

"Yea! Hurray!" We tumbled out of the car. Mrs. Pike parked next to us, and the triplets and Vanessa tumbled out of her car. The Pike kids were all jumping around and yelling. No wonder. The air smelled *wonderful.* It wasn't just the salt. It was something else that I couldn't describe, a freshness that was different from country air.

"We're back, we're here, we've come once more, to our gingerbread house by the white seashore!" sang Vanessa.

"Hey, that was a good one," said Byron appreciatively.

I took a look at the Pikes' rented house. We were facing the back, but even from there I could see that it *was* sort of gingerbready — with carved railings and posts and eaves and edges. Very old-fashioned. It was large and rambling, painted yellow with white trim. I glanced at Mary Anne and could tell that she had already fallen in love with it. I knew she was mentally writing a postcard to Dawn, describing the house and its view of the ocean.

"Do you rent the same house every year?" I asked Mallory as we unloaded cartons from the car.

"Yup," she said. "And we're so lucky. I mean, right on the beach and everything. In the evening we sometimes sit on the front porch and just stare out at the ocean. And when it rains. . . ."

"Yeah?"

"I go up to this room on the third floor and sit on this window seat and watch the lightning and the waves crashing and everything."

I shivered. It sounded very romantic.

"Plus," added Mallory, "the lifeguard stand is right in front of our house. We can walk out the front door and straight into the ocean for a swim."

The driveway was behind the house, and we were carrying things in through the back door. Inside, Mrs. Pike was directing traffic.

"Why don't you take the same rooms you had last year?" she suggested. "Boys in the big bedroom at the end of the hall. Claire and Margo, in the room next to Daddy and me. Vanessa and Mallory, the pink bedroom. Oh, and Mal, show Mary Anne and Stacey the yellow bedroom, okay?"

Mary Anne was looking around the house, wide-eyed. The rooms on the first floor were big and bright and airy. I saw a living room, a sunporch, and a kitchen before Mallory whisked us up the wide staircase to the second floor.

The second floor consisted of a hallway,

bedrooms, and bathrooms. It reminded me a little of Watson's house, only it wasn't nearly as big. Mallory opened a door toward the end of the hall.

"This is the yellow bedroom," she said. "If you don't like it, there are a couple of rooms on the third floor, or you could trade with somebody."

"Oh, no, it's perfect!" Mary Anne breathed. "Just perfect."

It was a pretty room, I suppose, although not really to my taste. It was old-fashioned, with two high, dark wood beds, a bare wood floor, and yellow flowered wallpaper. It did, however, have a view of the beach. Out our window was sand and sun and the lifeguard stand.

"This is great!" I said to Mary Anne as soon as Mallory had left. "What a view. Come on, let's unpack. Then we can help the kids unpack, and after lunch, we can go out and do something."

We did just that. We emptied our suitcases, putting things in the tall bureau between our beds, or hanging them in the closet. Then we gave the Pike kids a hand. While Mr. and Mrs. Pike were still unpacking boxes and opening windows and making grocery lists, Mary Anne and I made sandwiches and served them up at the table in the kitchen.

As we were finishing lunch, I made the mistake of asking, "So what do you guys want to do this afternoon?"

"Go to the beach," said Mallory.

"Go to the arcade," said Jordan.

"Go swimming," said Adam.

"Go to Trampoline Land," said Nicky.

"Make sandcastles," said Claire.

"Go on the Ferris wheel," said Margo.

"Go to Ice-Cream Palace," said Byron, who loves to eat.

"Look for shells, look for shells, washed to shore by the ocean swells," (That was Vanessa, obviously.)

Mary Anne and I glanced at each other. Mary Anne raised her eyebrows. "Well," she said slowly, "maybe we can do everything . . . sort of."

"How?" asked the kids.

"Yeah, how?" I asked.

"We'll go exploring," replied Mary Anne. "Stacey and I haven't been here before. Why don't you take us on a tour? You can show us everything. We probably won't have time to go on rides or play games, but at least we can see the town."

The triplets were the first to okay the idea,

and the others quickly followed. Fifteen minutes later, Mary Anne and I were herding the Pike kids out the back door and down the street.

"Where do we start?" I asked.

"The main drag," replied Adam promptly.

"Yeah, that's good," said Mallory. "We'll walk right through town, and then go over to the boardwalk and come back home that way."

Walking "right through town" took just under two hours. At least one Pike wanted to stop at nearly every place we passed. Nicky wanted to see how much it cost to jump on the trampolines this summer. Byron wanted to see if the price of ice-cream cones was the same, and whether Ice-Cream Palace still had bing cherry vanilla. Mallory and Vanessa ducked into every souvenir shop along the way. They exclaimed over the little animals made of shells (which *were* pretty cute) and Sea City hats, towels, mugs, T-shirts, shorts, and postcards.

We almost had tears when we passed a penny candy store called Candy Heaven and Byron discovered two quarters in his pocket and started buying up — but only for himself. The others wanted candy, too. Luckily, Mary Anne and I had just enough change to buy each of them a jawbreaker. And Mary Anne bought a tiny chocolate teddy for herself, but

I had to go without, of course. When we left Candy Heaven, all you could hear was *slurp, slurp, slurp,* and exclamations of, "Mine's turning blue now!" or, "Hey, look! Mine's yellow!" or, "When mine gets smaller, I'm going to bite it in half and look at all the layers."

We proceeded along the main drag.

"There's Burger Garden!" said Byron, as we passed a tacky-looking restaurant. It was surrounded by a "garden" of plastic flowers. The eat-out tables were in the shape of mushrooms, and the waiters and waitresses were dressed like animals.

"Ask Claire what this place is called," whispered Jordan.

"What's this place called?" I asked her.

"Gurber Garden."

Jordan hooted. "She never says it right!"

We continued on our way. "There's Candy Kitchen," said Margo. "That's where we get fudge. It's yummy-yummy!"

"And there's miniature golf," pointed out Jordan.

"That looks like fun," I said. "They didn't have miniature golf in New York City. Have you ever played, Mary Anne?"

"A couple of times. There's a miniature golf course near Shelbyville in Connecticut."

I kept looking. I looked so long that Adam said hopefully, "Maybe we could play now."

"Sorry, kiddo," I told him. "I wish we could, too, but we don't have any money. I'm sure we'll come back, though. It would be fun to play sometime."

We stood around and watched a while longer. Then we continued with our exploring. It took us another hour to walk along the boardwalk, and finally we ended up on the beach in front of the Pikes' house.

"Can we go in the water?" asked Nicky.

I looked at my watch. "Nope. Sorry," I said. "It's five o'clock. The lifeguards are getting ready to leave. Besides, you guys aren't wearing your bathing suits."

"Can't we even go wading?" Nicky pressed.

"Please, please, please? Just to our knees?" added Vanessa.

"No," I told them. "You know the rules."

"You could make a sandcastle or look for shells," suggested Mary Anne.

Nicky pouted. "That's girl stuff," he announced. "I know. We'll play paddle ball." He ran into the house to get rackets and balls.

Mary Anne and I settled ourselves in the sand. We watched the rest of the Pike kids run around, laughing, glad to be at the seashore finally. I looked at the other people on the beach. They were mostly families. Then I watched the lifeguards. They had jumped off of their wooden stand and were pulling on blue windbreakers that said SEA CITY COMMUNITY BEACHES. One had dark, curly hair; the other wavy, blonde hair. They looked about seventeen years old.

As the blonde one leaned over to fold his towel, the sun caught his hair, making it gleam. And at that moment, he glanced up. He saw me looking at him, and gave me a smile and a little wink.

He was gorgeous. Absolutely gorgeous.

He turned back to his towel and I let out my breath in a shaky gasp.

"Oh, wow," I whispered to Mary Anne. "I'm in love."

"Huh?" she said, frowning.

"I'm in love," I repeated, "with that gorgeous lifeguard."

Mary Anne just shook her head. I knew she thought I was crazy.

Sunday

Dear Kristy,
Here's something for the notebook: Pikes get up early. See ya! Stacey

Sunday

Dear Claudia,
I'm in LUV with that blonde, tan hunk of a lifeguard! Today I found out his name. It's Scott. And I think he likes me. Later! Luv,
Stace

P.S. I can't let Mary Anne see this card. She doesn't understand about Scott at all. She thinks I'm looney tunes.

"Stacey?" whispered a small voice.

I pulled the covers over my head, hoping the small voice was part of a dream. It was Sunday morning. Very early Sunday morning. Something had awoken me from a sound sleep.

"Stacey?" whispered the voice again, more urgently.

"Mmphh."

"STACEY-SILLY-BILLY-GOO-GOO?"

"WHAT?" I sat up in bed like I'd been shot out of a cannon. "What is it?"

Margo was standing in the doorway to our bedroom. Claire was next to her.

"We want to go to the beach," said Margo.

"What's going on?" asked Mary Anne sleepily from across the room.

"These two want to go to the beach and it's the middle of the night," I said.

"No, it isn't," replied Margo. "The sun's almost up."

"Mr. Sun-silly-billy-goo-goo!" cried Claire.

"Shh, you guys. It's too early for the beach. It's even too early to get up. Come in bed with me."

The girls scrambled for my bed, but three of us were a tight squeeze, so Claire got in bed with Mary Anne instead. We all went back to sleep. We didn't wake up until we smelled breakfast cooking.

"Mmm," I mumbled. "Scrambled eggs. Bacon. Toast."

"Daggles-silly-billy-goo-goo is making breakfast," Claire announced.

Mary Anne and I got dressed and the four of us were downstairs in ten minutes. The other Pikes had gathered. Mallory and Adam were already in their bathing suits. But Nicky, Vanessa, Byron, Jordan and the little girls were still in their pajamas. I had a feeling it might take awhile to get eight kids ready for the beach.

"Good morning!" Mr. Pike greeted us. "I'm the chief cooker of breakfast around here. Are you hungry?"

"Starved!" Mary Anne and I replied.

"Good," he said. "Stacey, come give me a hand at the stove."

"I'm not much of a cook," I told him.

"That's all right," he replied when I'd reached his side. He lowered his voice. "I want to make sure you can eat what I'm fixing. The Danish is out, right?"

"Right," I said, looking longingly at a pan of sugary bakery Danish warming up in the oven. Cheese Danish used to be my favorite breakfast food.

"Toast?" he asked.

I read the ingredients on the bread wrapper. "That's okay," I told him.

"Bacon?"

"Fine."

"And the main course — cheese omelets," he said proudly.

"Oh. Um, no. It's the processed cheese. I can't eat it."

"No problem. I'll scramble you up a couple of plain eggs, okay?"

"Great," I replied. "Thanks."

Mr. Pike didn't look at all put out, but I felt terrible. A mother's helper wasn't supposed to create extra work for her clients. I began to feel apprehensive. What if Mallory or one of the younger Pike kids wanted to know why I was on a diet when I'm already pretty thin? But I put my fears aside, and felt better by the time breakfast was over and no one had mentioned my scrambled eggs or the fact that I had turned down "yummy-yummy" Danish in favor of plain old toast.

No sooner had the last bite of breakfast been eaten, than Jordan yelled, "Beach!" and the Pikes turned into a human tornado. Six of the kids needed to change into bathing suits. We had to find eight towels, two umbrellas, some chairs, four pails and shovels, four paddleball rackets and balls, books, a deck of cards, several tubes of sunscreen, T-shirts, and sodas. And that was just for the kids. Mary Anne and I had to get ourselves ready, too.

Mary Anne, ever-organized, had packed her beach bag the night before. Neatly arranged in it were a hairbrush, sunglasses, a headband, and a copy of *A Tree Grows in Brooklyn.* I threw together a similar bag, remembering to toss in the bottle of Sun-Lite. Then we prepared to peel off our shorts and shirts, revealing our bikinis.

"You first," I said to Mary Anne.

"No way. You first."

I'm not shy. I whipped off my clothes. Underneath was my new bikini. It was skimpy (and we're talking *very* skimpy) and yellow, with tiny bows at the sides on the bottom part. And if I do say so myself, the top part was filled out pretty nicely.

Mary Anne's eyes nearly bugged right off her face.

"Oh, my — " she started to say. "Well, that does it. I'm not taking *my* clothes off. I'll sit on the beach in a shirt and jeans. I'll wear an evening gown if I have to."

"Come on, Mary Anne," I said. "It can't be that bad. Let me see."

"No."

"Mary Anne, the kids are waiting. They want to hit the beach. They sound desperate. Off with your clothes."

Slowly Mary Anne removed her shirt and shorts. Underneath was a perfectly nice pale blue bikini with white stripes running diagonally across it. It wasn't quite as skimpy as mine, and the top wasn't filled out at *all* (Mary Anne and Kristy are just about the shortest, smallest girls in our grade), but she looked fine. I told her so.

Reluctantly, she helped get the kids organized. The ten of us struggled out the front door and across the sand. About halfway to the water, Mallory suddenly said, "This is a good place."

The kids dropped the junk they were holding and ran, leaving Mary Anne and me to set up our spot. It was nine-thirty and the lifeguards were on duty, so we knew the kids were pretty safe by the water. We spread out towels, opened the umbrellas, set out the beach chairs, and were ready.

I rubbed some Sun-Lite in my hair. "Sun, hit me with your rays," I said. I oiled myself up with sunscreen and sat back in a chair.

"Hey!" yelped Mary Anne. "We forgot to put lotion on the kids. They'll be as red as lobsters if we're not careful."

We had to round up all the kids and make sure they got lathered with sunscreen. Then we turned them loose again.

I put on my shades. I put on my visor. I sat back in my chair again. The sand was white and warm. The sky was a brilliant blue. In front of me, the ocean crashed and foamed. This was the life.

I gazed around. Not far away, a mother and three little kids were parked. In another spot were a mother, a father, a grandmother, and a little boy about Nicky's age. With some interest, I watched two boys, one about seven, one about four, tugging at the hands of an older boy (fourteen?) and pulling him impatiently along the beach. The older boy was trying to carry a bundle of towels, an umbrella, and a baby. They stopped near us. The boy reminded me of me. He spread out their towels, rubbed sunscreen on the children, and then let the boys run to the water while he stayed under the umbrella with the baby.

Was the boy their brother? I didn't think so. He was fair-skinned with light brown hair, while the children had olive complexions and masses of black curls.

I nudged Mary Anne. "See that boy over there?"

She nodded.

"I think he's a guy mother's helper."

"Really?"

For the next fifteen minutes or so, Mary Anne and I kept an eye on the Pike kids, watched the other mother's helper, and just enjoyed the beach. Of course, I had checked out the lifeguard stand. Two guys were on duty, and they were cute, but neither one was the hunk I'd seen the day before.

"Stacey?" said Mary Anne after a while. "Look at Byron."

I searched the shoreline. I saw Mallory, Jordan, Adam, and Nicky shrieking around in waist-high water. Claire, Margo, and Vanessa were crouched in the wet sand at the water's edge, making castles that were meant to be washed away with each wave. But Byron was hanging back, alone. He was sitting in dry sand, staring out to sea.

"What's wrong with him?" I wondered.

"He hasn't been near the water since we got here. He hasn't even stuck a toe in."

"He does know how to swim, doesn't he?"

"I know for a fact that he does. I remember when the triplets were taking lessons at the Y," replied Mary Anne.

My attention was drawn away from Byron by something very interesting. A jeep was driving up the beach. It stopped by the lifeguard stand. Two guys wearing windbreakers got out. One removed a pair of mirrored sunglasses. It was the hunk! Noskote and lipcoat were smeared on his face, but it didn't matter. He was as gorgeous as ever. He was totally cool!

And he was changing places with one of the guards on duty! The hunk was now sitting just ten yards away from me. Unfortunately, I was facing his back.

"There he is! There he is!" I hissed to Mary Anne.

"Who?" She was still watching Byron.

"Him! That incredible hunk from yesterday. The lifeguard of my dreams. Oh, I am in love with him for sure. I mean it."

"You're not the only one."

"Huh?"

"Look." Mary Anne pointed to a group of girls about our age who had gathered at the base of the lifeguard stand. They seemed to have materialized out of thin air. They were giggling and talking and asking the guards questions.

My heart sank.

All morning I watched the lifeguards and the girls. I watched them much more than I watched the Pike kids. Mary Anne seemed a bit miffed, but I couldn't help it. I was in love.

How did those other girls get so lucky? Not only did the lifeguards seem to know them, but they gave them the supreme honor of letting them do favors for them. Those girls got to bring them sodas and pick up anything that fell off the stand, and one was even asked to fix them sandwiches for lunch.

"Will you quit looking over there?" Mary Anne finally said crossly. "You're boy-crazy. Those lifeguards are much too old for you."

"They are not."

"Are too."

At that moment, three girls who were definitely in high school, maybe even in college, sauntered down the beach. The lifeguards stopped talking to the younger girls surrounding the stand, and watched the progress of the older ones with interest.

"See what I mean?" said Mary Anne smugly.

"Oh, cut it out," I snapped. "You don't understand."

And that was all we said to each other until we rounded up the Pikes for lunch and a little break from the hot sun. The kids ate hungrily but didn't want to stay inside for long. They were soon clambering to get back to the sea and sand. I made them all put on sweatshirts and things, since their skin wasn't used to the sun, and I put on some extra clothes myself.

(Only Mary Anne refused to do this. She said she wanted to get tan right away.) Then we ran out to the beach again. Mr. and Mrs. Pike decided to go into town.

The kids made a beeline for the water, despite the fact that I'd just told them not even to go wading until their lunches had had a chance to digest for an hour.

"At least Byron paid attention to you," Mary Anne pointed out.

"Yeah. . . . Uh-oh."

I jumped up. At the water's edge, Adam and Jordan were splashing Byron.

"Quit it!" he shouted. "Cut it out!"

"Sissy!" Adam yelled back.

"Jerk!"

"Baby!"

"Ratface!"

"Okay, okay, okay," I reached the boys in record time. "What's going on here?"

"He started it!" Byron cried.

"I don't care who started it. I want to know what you're fighting about."

Mary Anne had run up behind me. When Adam made a grab for Jordan, she dived between them, separating them and almost losing her bikini.

"Byron is a baby!" exclaimed Adam. "He won't go in the ocean."

"And you're mad at him for that?" I asked.

"I want him to come in with us. Triplets stick together. He's ruining everything."

"I guess the only choice is for the three of you to do something *out* of the water," Mary Anne pointed out practically, adjusting her bathing suit.

I turned around at that moment and saw the hunk watching us. He flashed me a grin. My knees melted. I just *had* to talk to him.

While Mary Anne took over with the triplets, I sauntered up to the lifeguard stand.

"Hey, cutie," said the hunk.

My knees practically disappeared, but I turned on all the charm I could find. "Do you have the time?" I asked. "My watch isn't working."

The group of girls around the stand looked at me warily. They backed off a couple of steps.

"Sure," replied the hunk. "It's two twenty-five."

"Thanks," I said.

Just as I was turning away, I heard a cry and the sound of sobbing. "Stacey!" shouted Mallory's voice.

Mallory ran to me, carrying Claire, whose foot was bleeding. "She cut it on a shell," said Mallory.

"WAHH! Stacey," wailed Claire, holding out her arms to me.

I reached for her — and realized that the hunk was at my side. He was holding a first-aid kit. In no time, he had cleaned Claire's cut and put a Band-Aid on it. Claire and I both gazed at him adoringly.

As Claire ran off a few moments later, the hunk said, "Maybe we better introduce ourselves. I'm Scott. Scott Foley. I've been noticing you."

(The girls at the stand retreated even farther.)

"I — I'm Stacey McGill," I told him. "Thirteen years old. Formerly of New York City." (Oh, I could just *die!* What a stupid thing to say.)

But Scott simply smiled again. "I better get back on duty," he said.

That afternoon, I talked to Scott several more times. I asked him about the weather for the next day. I asked when high tide would be. I pretended I really, really needed to know. Then, around four-thirty, Scott asked me if I'd mind getting him a soda. (*Mind?!*)

The girls left altogether. I had Scott to myself for the rest of the afternoon. I found out that he lived in Princeton, New Jersey, had recently turned eighteen, and was going to college in September. He *was* a little old for me, but I didn't care.

Just before supper that night, I escaped Mary

Anne's accusations about how little help I was being, and ran across the beach and down to the water's edge. I stared at the spot where the lifeguard stand had been, and then at the tracks it left as it had been dragged back to the dunes for the night. After a moment, I knelt down in the wet sand. I found a piece of shell and carefully printed:

STACEY + SCOTT = LUV

Then I ran back to the house before a wave came in. I didn't want to see the words wash away.

Chapter 6

Monday

Dear Kristy,

A problem with Nicky. The triplets think he's babyish, so they don't play with him. But there are no other boys in the family, and he doesn't like getting stuck with the girls, especially Vanessa. I feel kinda sorry for him.

Luv,
Stacey

Monday

Dear Dawn,

Hi! How is sunny California? Guess what? I am sunburned. I look like a tomato with hair.

Love,
Mary Anne

Mr. and Mrs. Pike spent almost all of Monday on the beach with the kids and Mary Anne and me.

Scott wasn't on duty.

I was depressed.

But I felt better that afternoon when Mrs. Pike said that she and Mr. Pike wanted to go out to dinner — just the two of them — to this fancy restaurant in Jamesport, the next town over, and gave Mary Anne and me enough to take the Pike kids out for the evening.

"Probably the best you'll be able to do with that is go to Burger Garden, which is fairly inexpensive, and get a treat on the boardwalk later," said Mrs. Pike.

At this, the kids became hysterical with joy.

"Gurber Garden-silly-billy-goo-goo!" exclaimed Claire.

"Burger Garden! What a way to end this bright and sunny day!" said Vanessa, who was sounding more like a greeting card with each poem.

The others cheered.

At six o'clock that evening we waved goodbye to Mr. and Mrs. Pike as they backed out of the driveway.

"Well, let's go!" said Jordan.

"I want a double Crazy Burger with the works," announced Byron.

The kids looked at Mary Anne and me expectantly.

"You're all ready to go?" I asked them.

"Yup."

"You're all wearing shoes?"

"Yup."

"You've all been to the bathroom?"

"Yup."

"Really?"

"Yup."

"Wait a sec," said Mary Anne. "Where's Vanessa?"

"In our room. She's still getting dressed, I think," said Mallory.

I ran upstairs to the pink bedroom. Vanessa was slowly getting herself ready. Sometimes I think that if Vanessa ever had to race the tortoise, she'd lose.

"Ready?" I asked her.

"Almost."

"Everyone's waiting."

"I know, I know," she said frantically. "I just can't go. My feet are moving much too slow."

I laughed. "Come on, slowpoke." I tied her shoelaces and hair ribbons and she was ready.

We set off for Burger Garden, Mary Anne and Mallory leading the way; the triplets, Claire, Margo, and Nicky in the middle; and Vanessa and me bringing up the rear.

Considering the appealing places we passed on the way — Candy Heaven, souvenir stands, the Ice-Cream Palace — we reached Burger Garden in pretty good time. The Pikes' excitement had been building with every step we took. As we approached the entrance, an explosion of chatter burst from them.

"We sit at mushrooms to eat!"

"Crazy Burgers have orange sauce on them 'cause the ketchup and mustard's already mixed together!"

"I want to ride the merry-go-round!"

"It's delightful, let's all blab it. The burgers here are served by a rabbit!"

"Last year there was a coloring contest and I won two Crazy Burgers and a Fantasy Fountain Soda!"

Mary Anne and I looked around. Burger Garden consisted of a very informal indoor restaurant where you could sit at either tables or a long counter with high stools, and an outdoor garden. Despite all the kids spinning happily on the stools, the garden was obviously the more fun place to eat.

The Pikes headed for it immediately.

"I wanna sit by the merry-go-round!" cried Claire.

"Shh," I said. "We'll sit wherever we're seated. And we'll probably need three tables."

"There are some empty mushrooms over by the Enchanted Tree," said a large mouse. The mouse was holding menus in her paws. "This way, please."

"Well, this is a first," whispered Mary Anne. "In fact, it's been a week of firsts. My first bikini, my first trip away from home, my first time at the Jersey Shore. And now, my first meal ever served by an animal."

I giggled. "Or eaten on a mushroom."

"By the Enchanted Tree, whatever that is," she added.

The mushrooms were sort of small, so we did need three. Claire and Margo ran to one and Vanessa sat down by herself. Then the triplets bunched up at the third mushroom. Nicky ran over to them.

"Go sit with Vanessa," Adam told Nicky.

"No, I want to sit with you."

"Us triplets are sitting alone," said Jordan.

"No, you're not, because I'm sitting with you," I said.

"No way!" cried Adam.

"Where will I sit?" exclaimed Nicky, downcast. "I'm not sitting with girls."

"Sit with us Nicky-silly-billy-goo-goo," said Claire.

"You're *girls,*" said Nicky disparagingly.

Vanessa was still at a table by herself. "Hey, what's the matter, what's the fuss, sit with me, I'll — "

"NO!" cried every single one of her brothers and sisters.

"We don't want to eat with Elizabeth Barrett Browning," said Mallory.

"Who's Elizabeth Barrett Browning?" asked Nicky.

"A poet."

"A very good one," Mary Anne pointed out.

"Well, anyway, we don't want to — " Nicky began.

"Look," I broke in suddenly, "a six-foot mouse has been waiting about five minutes for us to sit down. If you guys don't find places, we're never going to eat."

Everyone dove for the mushrooms. Against my better judgment, I let the triplets sit alone. Mary Anne sat down with Claire and Margo, and I joined Nicky, Vanessa, and Mallory. Before he allowed us to open our menus, Nicky made Vanessa promise not to rhyme a single word during the meal.

"Are you happy now?" I asked him.

"Yup."

We opened the menus and took a look. It's a good thing I like hamburgers because, except for hotdogs and chili, the only main dishes on the menu were burgers. Twenty different varieties.

After a few moments, a large rabbit stepped up to us. "Hi, I'm Bugs," he said. "Any questions about the menu?"

"What's the Surprise Burger today?" I asked.

"That would be the burger with tofu and avocado."

Vanessa nearly choked.

She and Nicky and Mallory and I ordered Crazy Burgers — burgers with bacon, Swiss cheese, pickles, and the orange sauce.

When Bugs moved on to the triplets, Nicky turned to me and said conversationally, "So one day this matta-baby comes up to me — "

"What's a matta-baby?" I interrupted.

"Nothing," replied Nicky. "Whatsa matta with you?" He pounded the table with glee.

Mallory rolled her eyes.

"Can I go see what the Enchanted Tree is?" asked Vanessa.

"Sure," I told her.

"It's — it's — you won't believe it!" she cried a few minutes later. She was running back to our mushroom. "It's just like in *Charlie and the Chocolate Factory!* That tree is growing chocolate bars!"

"Really?" asked Nicky, amazed.

"No, stupid. They're just hanging all over it. And they cost twenty-five cents apiece and so you buy one and if it has a gold wrapper inside you win a prize just like Charlie Bucket did only it's for Burger Garden food not the chocolate factory and I didn't rhyme a single word, Nicholas. So there."

Bugs came back and served us our drinks. At the next mushroom, the triplets shot their straw papers at each other.

"Well," I said loudly, turning to Mary Anne, "I guess I'll go sit with the triplets."

"No, no!" said Byron hastily. "We'll stop. Really."

And they did.

All the Pikes behaved themselves. When the food was served, they scarfed it up without messes or squabbles. Later, after Mary Anne and I had seen what the bill came to, we let each kid buy a candy bar from the Enchanted Tree. Nicky got a gold wrapper! It turned out to be worth four free Burger Garden dinners. Suddenly the triplets were his best friends.

Mary Anne and I counted the remaining money and debated how to spend the rest of the evening. We decided to go to the boardwalk for a while and then back to the Ice-Cream Palace before heading home.

On the boardwalk, we gave each kid a dollar to spend, all we thought we could afford, not knowing how expensive the Palace might be. The kids planned and planned, each wanting to get the best and the most for his or her money. The only thing we said they couldn't do was go on fast rides. I was not about to watch anybody throw up a Crazy Burger.

An hour later, Byron had ridden the Ferris wheel twice; Vanessa had bought a little pink deer from the glass blower; Claire, Nicky, and Margo had tried the bumper cars; Mallory had bought a frog made out of seashells; and Jordan and Adam had been through the haunted house, and were mad at Byron, who had refused to go with them.

We arrived at the Ice-Cream Palace feeling ready to sit down for a while.

"Okay," I said, "I'm not going to have any ice cream, so that means there's about three dollars for each of you." I was eyeing the menu. The Palace looked expensive.

"More than three," spoke up Mary Anne. "I — I don't think I'll have any, either."

"What's wrong?" I asked warily. "You look kind of funny."

"I don't know. I feel sort of hot all over."

"Your face is awfully red," I said.

"My skin feels stiff."

"Your *skin* feels — Just a second. Hold out your arms."

Mary Anne obliged.

I pressed her skin with my finger. A white spot appeared where my finger had been. It slowly turned bright pink — like the rest of her skin. "You're sunburned!" I exclaimed. "Eat some ice cream. It'll probably cool you off."

We had enough money for everyone to have what he or she wanted, with two dollars and thirty-one cents left over.

We got back to the beach house shortly after nine. Mr. and Mrs. Pike were still out.

"You are *so* sunburned!" Mallory exclaimed to Mary Anne.

"Oh, I know. Don't remind me."

Mary Anne flopped down on her bed. She lay on her back with her arms stretched out, while I looked on helplessly. "What did I do to deserve this?" she moaned.

She'd been lying there for about ten minutes while the kids were supposed to be getting ready for bed, when a voice said, "Mary Anne? I brought you something."

"We all did," said another voice.

Standing in the doorway were the Pike kids, each in pajamas, each holding something out to Mary Anne.

"It's for your sunburn," said Margo. "I brought you Noxema."

"I brought you Solarcaine," said Byron.

"An ice pack," said Jordan.

"Cold compresses," said Adam.

"Mom's aloe creme," said Vanessa.

"A fan," said Nicky. "To cool off."

"Teabags for your eyelids," said Mallory. "They really work."

"Butter," said Claire, offering Mary Anne a tub of margarine.

"Butter is for *real* burns, not sunburns!" screeched Nicky. He grabbed for his little sister, but Claire twisted away and fled to Mary Anne. Nicky followed. So did everyone else. They ended up on Mary Anne's bed in a giggly heap — margarine, ice, and all. I joined them.

I don't think I've ever laughed so hard in my life.

Tuesday

Dear Claudia,

I know I'm supposed to be baby-sitting, but Scott was on duty today, and he's all I can think of. He gave me the most fabulous present, but I'm not going to tell you what it is. I'll show you when we're back in Stoneybrook. Say "hi" to Mimi!

Luv, Stace

P.S. Mary Anne thinks the gift is dumb. She doesn't understand.

Tuesday

Dear Kristy,

I'd never have suspected it, but Byron has a lot of fears. He's afraid to go in the ocean (even though he can swim), and last night when we went to the amusement park on the boardwalk, he wouldn't go through the haunted house. We'll have to talk about this.

Luv, Stacey

On Tuesday, the weather was pretty. The beach looked like a postcard. Mary Anne and I took the kids out early, even before Scott was on duty. The air was cool, the sky was crystal clear with one or two fluffy white clouds that looked sort of like sheep, and the sun was all sparkly, but not hazy and blazy the way it would get during the afternoon.

Mary Anne came to the beach that morning wearing a long-sleeved caftan and a Boston Red Sox cap that Adam had lent her. She looked pretty weird — even weirder after she gooped on Noskote and lipcoat, then put on her sunglasses. As an added precaution, she sat under the umbrella. I didn't say anything. I knew she felt hot and uncomfortable.

The second the lifeguards showed up, the kids (except for Byron, of course) dashed into the water. I sauntered after them, supposedly to keep an eye on them, but really as an excuse to say hello to Scott. He greeted me with, "Hey there, princess."

I thought I might pass out.

"Hi," I said. "Was yesterday your day off?"

"Sure was. I used it well, too."

I added that bit of information — *Monday is Scott's day off* — to my mental list of things I knew about him. I wished the list were longer.

Then I leaned casually against the lifeguard stand, almost as if I was posing. I glanced across the beach to see if Mary Anne was watching. But she was busy. Claire, Margo, and Vanessa, already dripping wet, were crowded around her, asking her to help them with something. And to my surprise, the guy mother's helper was leaning over behind Mary Anne, giving her a hand.

I didn't have time to think about that, though. Right then, things started happening pretty quickly.

First, a couple of the other girls showed up. "Hi, Scott," they said.

"Do you kids know Stacey McGill?" he asked.

Kids! He had called them kids! He must have thought I acted older than they did!

That was all the girls needed to hear. Scowling, they edged around to the other side of the lifeguard stand. "Hi, Bruce," said one, giggling.

"Hey, beautiful," replied Bruce.

More giggling.

I had Scott to myself again.

I looked back at our towels. Mary Anne was alone.

I was just about to check around for Claire and Margo when it happened.

"SHARK!" yelled a terrified voice from out in the waves.

In one second, Scott and Bruce were on their feet, binoculars to their eyes. Then they put the binoculars down, glanced at each other, nodded, and began whistling people in.

FWEEEET! "Everybody in! Everybody in!"

FWEEEET! "Outta the water!"

Then Scott blew three short *fweets* and signaled to the guards down the beach, while Bruce signaled to the ones up the beach.

I've never seen people move so fast. Those in the ocean staggered out. Those on the beach ran to the water's edge. Frantically, I tried to round up the Pikes. I gathered Byron, Jordan, Nicky, and Vanessa in a matter of seconds.

"Mary Anne!" I yelled, spotting her caftan and baseball cap. "Where are the rest of the kids? We have to make sure they haven't . . . I mean — " I didn't want to say, Haven't been eaten alive by some relative of Jaws.

"I've got Claire and Adam."

"Oh, no! We're missing Mallory and Margo!"

"No, you're not. Here we are," said Mallory, running up to me, pulling Margo along.

"Oh, thank goodness."

Mary Anne and I counted the Pikes about five times before we were satisfied that they were all safe and sound.

"I want to see the shark!" cried Nicky, jumping up and down.

So did I. "Okay," I said. "Let's walk down the beach, away from this crowd."

Mary Anne and the other kids followed us. When we had a little space, we held our hands to our eyes, blocking the glare of the sun, and stared out to sea.

"I think I see something!" exclaimed Byron.

"Where?" we all asked.

He pointed. "See? Sort of over to the left?"

I could make out a faraway shape, but it looked like a sea gull bobbing on the waves.

Later, Adam swore he could see five fins circling around, but nobody else saw them. At last we gave up. We walked back to the lifeguard stand.

The crowd was dispersing. Scott and Bruce were back on duty. I saw a good opportunity to ask Scott a question.

"Hi," I said to him, leaning against the base of the stand and squinting up.

"Hi, love."

Love! Scott had called me love! Of course, he meant *his* love.

When I recovered, I managed to say, "So were there really sharks?"

"It looked that way. Sometimes it's hard to tell, but it's better to be safe than sorry."

"I'll say."

Scott wiped his brow. "It's going to be a hot one."

"So you want a soda or something?" I asked eagerly.

"You bet, love. That'd be great."

I was off in a flash. I didn't even remember to tell Mary Anne where I was going. I grabbed a soda out of the Pikes' fridge, ran back across the sand, and handed the ice-cold can to Scott.

He held it against his forehead. "Oh, wow. That feels great," he said. Then he popped open the can, tipped his head back, drank half the can without stopping, and handed it to Bruce. Bruce finished it off practically in one gulp.

"That sure hit the spot, honey," said Scott.

I was dying. I was *dying!*

After lunch that day, Mary Anne and I stood at the water's edge. I alternately tried to coax Byron into the water (he staunchly refused, saying he didn't want to be eaten by a shark) and found excuses to talk to Scott. Every time I did, I noticed Mary Anne giving me dirty looks.

Well, could I help it if Scott needed a sandwich and then another soda? I'm sorry if she thought she had her hands full, but it wasn't *my* fault Adam dumped a bucket of water over Byron, or that Nicky disappeared for ten minutes. It turned out he'd gone back to the house without telling anyone, but Mary Anne panicked. She was just going to have to learn to cope with things like that.

At five o'clock, Scott and Bruce climbed down from their stand. Mary Anne called the Pike kids out of the water. "I think we should take them inside," she said to me. "Mallory and Jordan look kind of burned. And I know Claire's tired."

"Okay, you start," I told her. "I want to talk to Scott for a minute."

"*Sta*cey," she said impatiently, "there are two umbrellas, ten towels, a set of Tonka toys, buckets, shovels, card games, suntan lotion, and beach bags to pack up."

"Well, you've got eight kids to help you," I pointed out. "Besides, I'll be there in a minute."

"You're getting paid as much as I am," said Mary Anne in a huff, "and *I'm* doing all the work."

Since she was sunburned, I forgave her.

Anyway, the guy mother's helper turned up to give her a hand. I realized that he had helped her look for Nicky earlier, too. So what was she complaining about?

While Mary Anne rounded up the Pikes, I

watched Scott get ready to leave. Then I followed him as he and Bruce dragged the stand back to the dunes.

"Well," I said after a moment, "I guess I'll see you tomorrow."

The lifeguard jeep was driving up the beach to pick them up.

"Just a sec, Stacey," said Scott. "Hey, man, you go on to the jeep," he told Bruce. "I'll be right there."

Did Scott want to be alone with me?!

Scott flashed me his hunk grin. Then he lifted his whistle from around his neck and handed it to me by the chain. "You sure were a lifesaver today, princess," he said. "Thanks a lot. I want you to have my whistle."

I held it with shaking hands.

"Well," said Scott softly. "I better go. See you tomorrow?"

"Yeah. Tomorrow. Definitely. Hey, and thanks, Scott. This is really special."

I watched Scott run across the beach to the jeep and vault inside without opening the door.

I knew he had meant to say more to me, but was too shy. Boys get that way sometimes. Anyway, he didn't need words to tell me what he meant. I already knew.

Scott was in love with me!

Thursday

Dear Kristy,

Today the weather was awful. Stacey and I must have been out of our minds: we took the kids to the miniature golf course. But guess what? We had a great time. Sometimes I think that eight kids aren't any harder to take care of than two or three. The Pikes argue and tease, but they also help each other out.

Love,
Mary Anne

P.S. Stacey is being a real pain. She really is.

P.P.S. (Don't _ever_ show this card to her.)

I guess we should have expected at least one rainy day while we were in Sea City, but the weather had been so nice that somehow we didn't. So we were all kind of shocked when we woke up on Thursday, shivering in our beds, to find a misty, gray sky and cool, damp air. It wasn't actually raining, but it was certainly no beach day. In fact, by nine-thirty the beach was still deserted and we realized that the lifeguards weren't even going to go on duty. Why couldn't this have happened on Scott's day off? I wondered.

"I think," said Mr. Pike at breakfast that morning, "that today would be a good day to go to Smithtown."

"Oh, Dad, please. No. Not Smithtown," said Jordan, amid groans from his brothers and sisters.

"What's Smithtown?" asked Mary Anne.

"It's a dumb old town that's supposed to look like the seventeen-hundreds or something," said Adam.

"I always wear a frown when I go to Smithtown," added Vanessa.

"You've only been there once, honey," her mother pointed out.

"Once was enough," Byron whispered to Adam.

"Smithtown," said Mr. Pike, "is a very nice restored colonial village. There are stores and houses, a church, a blacksmith shop, crafts-people. . . ."

"Really?" said Mary Anne. That was just the kind of thing that would interest her.

"But you kids don't have to go if you don't want to," said Mrs. Pike.

"Oh, thanks, Mom," said Mallory. "Are you and Dad going to go anyway?"

Mr. and Mrs. Pike looked at each other. "Why not?" said Mr. Pike. "Can you kids find something to do today?"

"Oh, sure," I replied. "No problem."

(Mary Anne looked disappointed.)

So a little while later, Mr. Pike gave Mary Anne and me some money and he and Mrs. Pike drove off.

An hour after that, we were all bored silly. I'd written to my parents and my friend Laine in New York, and was tired of writing. There was no TV in the house, and the kids had already read, colored, and tried to invent a game of tag they could play indoors without breaking anything. Mallory had been up on the third floor, watching the angry ocean from the windowseat, but was tired of it. Every suggestion Mary Anne or I made was met with a bored "nah."

"Well," I said. "It's not actually raining. We could go into town or to the boardwalk."

"Yea!" cried the kids.

"*If*," said Mary Anne, "you promise to wear jackets or sweat shirts."

"We promise."

It wasn't easy, but the ten of us agreed on one thing we all wanted to do: play miniature golf.

It was late morning when we reached Fred's Putt-Putt Course. Because of the weather, a lot of other people had had the same idea we'd had, and Fred's was kind of crowded. There was a short line of people waiting at almost every hole.

The kids were undaunted.

"Come on. Let's get our putt-putt clubs," cried Byron.

"I want a five-iron," said Nicky.

"Silly," said Mallory, smiling. "You get putt-putt clubs according to your height. There are no five-irons or anything."

"Silly-billy-goo-goo," added Claire.

I rolled my eyes.

When we were all equipped with our golf clubs, we lined up at the first hole. The par was four. That means the average person needs four strokes to hit the ball through the moving arms of a windmill, around a corner, and into a little sunken cup.

Claire insisted on going first. Twenty-seven strokes later, her ball was in the cup. There were nine more of us to play. The people behind us, a man and a woman, began to look impatient.

"Mind if we play through?" asked the man. "There are just the two of us. It'll only take a few minutes."

"No," cried Margo. "It's my turn! I want to go next!"

"Margo — " I said.

"That's all right," the man said to her. "You go on."

After Margo had tried eleven times to get her ball through the windmill, I thought the man would turn purple. Jordan told her she could pick it up and carry it to the other side.

"You go on through — sir," I said when Margo was finished.

"Thanks," he said with relief. He and the woman sped through expertly.

The older kids were somewhat better players. Mallory actually got her ball in the cup in the suggested four strokes. Even Mary Anne and I couldn't do that.

"Hey, you're good!" I said to Mallory.

"It was beginner's luck," muttered Byron, who'd taken twelve strokes.

The second hole looked a little easier. At the top of a short green ramp sat a clown's face with a blinking red nose. You were supposed to hit your ball into the clown's mouth, and it would come out of one of three holes on the other side. If it came out of the middle holc, you could get a hole in one — which is just what Nicky got.

"A hole in one! A hole in one!" he shrieked. "I did it! I never got a hole in one before."

Several people nearby smiled at him.

Adam had just scored an embarrassing ten on the clown hole. Nevertheless, he punched Nicky affectionately on the shoulder. "Good going, little bro," he said.

Nicky beamed.

The people behind us — a family, now — were beginning to get that look that the man and woman had had earlier. I called Mary Anne and Mallory over to me. "I think," I said, glancing nervously at the impatient family, "that we better split into three groups and play separately. Otherwise, we're likely to get killed." After much discussion, Mallory agreed to play with the triplets, Mary Anne took Nicky and Vanessa, and I took Claire and Margo.

We lined up at the third hole, which had a

royal theme and was called "Old King Cole Hole." Mallory and the triplets played through first, and went on to the fourth hole. A half hour later, they were waiting in line for the eighth hole, Mary Anne's group was playing the sixth hole, and Claire was taking her thirty-seventh stroke at "Old King Cole."

"Claire . . . dear," I said as sweetly as I knew how.

"What, Stacey-silly-billy-goo-goo?"

But before I could finish (and I hadn't even been sure what I was going to say), Margo interrupted.

"You know what I think?" she said. "I think we should make a limit. You can't hit the ball more than twenty times. Twenty is it. If you get to twenty, your turn is over."

I raised my eyebrows. Great suggestion!

But Claire was frowning. "What if my ball isn't in the cup yet?" she asked.

"Twenty would be a better score," I told her. "Remember, you don't want a lot of points. The person with the *fewest* points is the winner."

"Well, okay," said Claire.

The twenty-stroke limit made a big difference. Even so, by the time Mallory and the triplets were finished, we were only on the tenth hole, and Mary Anne was on the thirteenth. We let the older kids leave to look in stores, if they promised to stay nearby and not cross the busy main drag. When Mary Anne and Nicky and Vanessa finished, they joined the others.

Then it was just me, Margo, Claire, and the putt-putt course. We were on the fourteenth hole. There were four more to go — five if you counted the "nineteenth" hole, which was really just a fancy way to return your ball to the rental shop.

On the fifteenth hole, Claire dropped her putt-putt club on the green. "I'm *tired* of this, Stacey. I don't *wanna* play anymore." (She had just found out that her score was over two hundred.)

On the sixteenth hole, Margo did the same thing.

I didn't care. I was very tired of miniature golf, myself. "Okay," I said. "We just have to return our balls."

I led the girls to the nineteenth hole. Mallory had explained how it worked. You hit your ball up a ramp, it disappeared over the top, and ran down a chute back to Fred.

Thwack! My golf ball disappeared.

Thwack! Margo's ball disappeared.

Thwack! Claire's ball disappeared.

Then, *ding, ding, ding! Whoop, whoop, whoop!*

The second Claire's ball sailed into the chute, lights flashed, bells rang, sirens wailed. Fred came rushing out of his shop.

"Congratulations!" he exclaimed. "Somebody has just won two free games here!"

"Me! Me! Oh, it was *me!*" Claire cried, jumping up and down.

"You're the lucky five-hundredth person to return your golf ball this week." Fred handed Claire two tickets for free putt-putt.

"Oh, please, Stacey, can Margo and I play again right now?" asked Claire.

I looked at the lines of people and "Old King Cole" and the swinging putt-putt clubs.

I was beginning to get a headache.

"Claire," I said, "you can use your tickets on the next rainy day."

"Okay," she said. "But you know what, Stacey? You're a silly-billy-goo-goo."

"You know what, Claire? You are, too."

Claire slipped her hand in mine, and she and Margo and I went off to find the others.

Sunday

Dear Mary Anne and Stacey,

You will not believe what happened while I was taking care of David Michael, Andrew, and Karen this morning. It was a baby-sitter's nightmare. It all began when Watson told us he wanted his car washed. This is a warning, you guys. Never, never, ever, ever, EVER let little kids wash a car by themselves. This should be a Baby-sitters Club rule....

Kristy Thomas had been getting an awful lot of mail from Claudia and Dawn and Mary Anne and me — at least three postcards every day. And finally Mary Anne and I got a letter from her.

Believe it or not, we were all baby-sitting. Back in her old neighborhood in California, Dawn was sitting for some of the families she used to sit for. Claudia and her family had traveled to an isolated mountain resort. Although it was quiet — the perfect place for Mimi to recover from her stroke — a lot of other families were staying there, too. Claudia had sat for a couple of them.

Of course Kristy was in baby-sitters' heaven. She was the only club member left in Stoneybrook, so she had all our clients to herself. But her most memorable baby-sitting job during the two weeks we were apart was not for another family, but for her very own stepsister and stepbrother, six-year-old Karen and four-year-old Andrew, and her little brother, David Michael.

Kristy's long letter told us about the entire incident. It began on Sunday morning when Watson Brewer announced that he and Elizabeth (Kristy's mom) were going to spend the day at an estate auction. Kristy didn't know what that was, and didn't ask.

Then her older brothers, Sam and Charlie, announced that they were going back to the old neighborhood to visit friends for the day.

"I guess you're in charge then, Kristy," said her mother. "Can you baby-sit?"

"Sure," Kristy replied. She turned to David Michael, Karen, and Andrew. "What do you guys want to do today?"

"I'm busy," said David Michael. "Linny Papadakis is having a dog show. I'm entering Louie. Hey, do you want to come with me?"

"Yes," said Karen.

"No," said Andrew. (Andrew likes Louie all right, but he's afraid of most other dogs.)

"Karen, you can go to the dog show with David Michael," Kristy told her. "You could play with Hannie." (Hannie, Linny's younger sister, is a friend of Karen's.)

"That's okay. I'll stay with Andrew."

David Michael looked a little hurt, but didn't say anything.

Watson spoke up then. "I've got a job to be done," he said. "I need someone to wash the Ford."

"Oh, we'll do it! We'll do it!" shouted Karen.

"Can we use the hose and those big sponges? We'll do a great job, Daddy! Andrew and Kristy and I. We'll get your car cleaner than anything!"

The Ford is no big deal as cars go. In fact, it's sort of an emergency car. It's this old black thing that Watson used to drive years and years ago. He keeps it parked in a shed at the back of the property. (In his garage are a red sportscar and a fancy new car and the Thomases' green station wagon.) But Watson won't give the Ford away. He says you never know when you might need it. Kristy pointed out, though, that in all the time she's known Watson, he's washed the Ford twice, and driven it once.

But she didn't care. Car washing would be a good project for Andrew and Karen. So before everyone left that day, Watson drove the Ford out of the shed and parked it in the drive. Then he and Kristy's mother drove off in the sportscar, Sam and Charlie drove off in the station wagon, and David Michael led Louie, his fur brushed, his special plaid collar in place, over to the Papadakises'.

"Well?" said Kristy to Karen and Andrew. "Should we start?"

"Yea! Yea!" Karen jumped up and down.

"Okay," said Kristy. "First off, we put on

our bathing suits. Then we get everything we're going to need."

Twenty minutes later, the three of them were standing on the drive amid buckets, sponges, cloths, and soap.

"All right, Andrew. Let 'er rip!" called Kristy.

Andrew twisted the nozzle of the hose. A fine spray shot out. But they had no more than gotten the hood of the car wet when David Michael came slowly up the driveway with Louie. Louie was limping and David Michael was crying.

Kristy dropped her sponge and ran over to them. "David Michael, what happened?" she exclaimed.

David Michael could barely speak. "I (sob) — at the dog show (hiccup) — a big dog came (sniff) — and (hic) — he growled at Louie (sob) — and Louie growled back (sniffle) — and the dog showed his teeth (hic) — and Louie showed *his* teeth (sob) — and the big dog ran at Louie (hiccup) — and Louie ran away (sniff) — and cut his foot on something (hic, sob, sniffle)."

Kristy examined Louie's foot. Sure enough the pad was bleeding. The cut looked pretty big. "Well," said Kristy, "we better bring Louie inside and figure out what to do. Come on, you guys," she said to Andrew and Karen.

"No, we want to wash the car," cried Karen. "We can do it ourselves. Really."

Kristy looked doubtfully at the kids. Then she thought, What could go wrong? It's a black car. If they don't get it very clean, no one will notice.

"Will you remember to keep the windows *closed?*" she asked.

"Yes."

"And don't spray anything but the car."

"Okay."

"And don't rinse out the sponges in the garden. The soap'll kill the plants."

"We won't."

After a few more instructions, Kristy took Louie and David Michael inside. She spread out a towel for Louie and gave David Michael some lemonade. Then she tried to clean Louie's paw.

"I think we better call the vet," she said after a few minutes. "Maybe Dr. Smith will make a house call."

Dr. Smith, of course, did not make house calls.

So Kristy began phoning around the old neighborhood, trying to track down Charlie, since he could drive. While she was on the telephone, she noticed that Karen and Andrew ran in and out of the house a couple of times, but she didn't pay much attention.

Kristy finally reached Charlie at his friends the Ackermans', and he said he'd come right home. So Kristy made one more call — to the vet to say that Louie would be on his way out there soon. Then she decided she better check on Karen and Andrew. She went out the back door and approached the car from behind. It was just after noon and the sun was shining brightly. The Ford was gleaming.

"We're done, Kristy!" cried Andrew.

"Yup, we sure are," said Karen. "I bet the car has never looked so shiny."

Kristy had to agree. The car looked shiny all right. In fact, it looked kind of . . . silvery.

Kristy's heart sank, but she managed to ask, "What, um, did you two wash this car with?"

"Oh," said Karen proudly, "we didn't use the sponges. They were no good. We used something better. These. Daddy always uses them to get pots shiny." Karen held out two pieces of steel wool.

"Oh, *no,*" murmured Kristy. At last she dared to inspect the car closely. It was covered with big silvery-gray patches where the paint had been scrubbed away. "You guys!" Kristy shouted. "You took the paint off! You can't wash a car with steel wool. Your dad wanted the Ford clean, not naked. Oh, no! What are we going to do?"

Kristy was a nervous wreck. As the afternoon wore on, Charlie came home and drove Louie and David Michael to the vet. Kristy cleaned up the mess in the driveway. She got herself, Karen, and Andrew dressed again. Louie returned with three stitches in his paw.

And then . . . Watson and Kristy's mom came home. They'd bought two crystal champagne glasses at the estate sale, which they brought inside and showed off proudly.

"Watson?" Kristy began, just as Watson said, "How did the car washing go? We didn't look at the Ford yet."

Kristy, Karen, and Andrew glanced at one another guiltily. "I think you better look now," said Kristy.

They all trooped outside. Kristy explained what had happened.

"Oh, no!" gasped Kristy's mother.

Watson turned slightly pale.

"I'm really sorry," said Kristy. "I should have been watching the kids more closely."

"I'm afraid I have to agree with you," replied Watson. "I know you had an emergency, but you *were* in charge, and you *should* have been keeping a closer eye on them. In a way it's all right, though. See, I'd been thinking of having the car painted. I've always wanted a purple car. But there was no real excuse to paint the Ford since we hardly ever drive it. Now I have an excuse."

"Paint the car?" repeated Karen with a gleam in her eye. "Can Andrew and I paint it? That would be fun."

Watson, Kristy, and Kristy's mother fixed their eyes on her.

"No," said Kristy's mother.

"Absolutely not," said Watson.

"When chickens have lips," said Kristy.

And that was the end of the car wash.

K—

Sun.

Noth. new to rept. Kids fine. B. still afrd. of H_2O.

—S.

Sunday

Dear Claudia,

The most awful, humiliating thing in the world has happened. I can't believe it. I feel like such a jerk. Mary Anne tried to warn me about Scott but I wouldn't listen. She told me he was older. She told me this, she told me that. And I wouldn't listen. Oh, I am such a jerk. (I guess I've run out of room. I'll tell you the rest in the next postcard.)

Luv, Stace

I had to write *three* more postcards in order to tell Claudia the whole story. See, what had happened was completely unexpected — at least, it was unexpected to me.

We'd been in Sea City just over a week. I was having the time of my life. My hair was about two shades lighter, thanks to the sun, the salt, and of course my bottle of Sun-Lite. My skin was turning nice and brown. I had actual tan lines at the edges of my bikini. I also had another new bikini. I'd bought it on the main drag one afternoon. It was pink, with palm trees and parrots all over it.

(Mary Anne had gotten rid of her sunburn, but she didn't have much of a tan. The only thing that happened when she sat in the sun was that her skin turned sort of blotchy and pink. So she covered up on the beach and stayed under the umbrella as much as possible.)

I wasn't having a bit of trouble with my diabetes, either. I'd been able to stay on my diet, and my mother had only called twice to see how I was doing. The Pike kids hadn't paid any more attention to that than they had to the fact that I never joined them in ice cream or candy or breakfast doughnuts. The best thing, though, was Scott. The bad weather had cleared up, and I saw him both Friday and Saturday.

On Saturday Mr. and Mrs. Pike decided to go to Atlantic City for the day, so Mary Anne and I were on our own with the kids. But by the end of the day, she practically wasn't speaking to me. She accused me of spending too much time with Scott.

Personally, I think she was jealous. And if I were Mary Anne, I'd have been jealous, too. That nerdy mother's helper had been hanging around her endlessly, and the two of them were always doing stuff with the kids, like building sand castles, or collecting shells to make a moat around the towels and umbrellas.

Mary Anne says I'm not spending enough time with the children, but I *am* doing something important when I'm on the beach. I post myself by the lifeguard stand and watch the kids when they're in the water — and Adam and Jordan are in the water nonstop. I can't help it if Scott talks to me every now and then, or asks for a soda or something.

"Sweetheart," he said to me on Saturday afternoon, "did anyone ever tell you you're beautiful?"

Immediately, my heart began to beat faster.

"No," I replied, which wasn't quite true.

My parents are always telling me I'm beautiful, but they don't count. A blonde-haired, blue-eyed, tanned, muscled eighteen-year-old hunk certainly counts, though.

Scott smiled down at me. He started to say something then, but suddenly he jumped up, blowing his whistle.

FWEET! FWEET! "You're too far out!" *FWEET!* "Too far out!"

"What were you going to say?" I asked him when the excitement was over.

"Oh," replied Scott, "you're — you're the greatest."

See? I thought. He wants to say more, but he's just too shy.

I wished Mary Anne had been saying a little more. Later that afternoon when I asked her if she wanted a soda, she just shrugged.

"I'll go back to the house and get you a really cold one," I offered.

"No, thanks."

"Well, I'm going to get one for me."

"'Kay."

I paused. Then, "See you," I said.

Those were the last words we spoke to each other for the rest of the afternoon.

Mr. and Mrs. Pike returned from Atlantic City in a great mood.

"How would you like the evening off?" Mrs. Pike asked Mary Anne and me.

"We'd love it," I said. I tried to sound excited, but it was hard with Mary Anne so mad at me.

"Why don't you change out of your bathing suits right now?" Mrs. Pike went on. "We'll let you off the hook until ten o'clock tonight. You can join us for dinner — "

"We're going back to Burger Garden so I can get my free meals!" interrupted Nicky.

" — or you can go somewhere on your own," Mrs. Pike finished.

"We'll think about it while we change," I said. "Come on, Mary Anne!"

We flew upstairs to our room. "Mary Anne, please don't be mad," I said. "It's only five o'clock. We have five whole hours to ourselves. We could go to the boardwalk, eat supper, hang around, shop."

Mary Anne began to look a teeny bit interested. And by the time our bikinis were off, we had showered, and our boardwalk clothes were on, she was actually speaking to me.

We selected our outfits carefully. Who knew who we might see on the boardwalk at night. Cute guys . . . Scott. . . . I put on a white cotton vest over a pink cotton dress and tied a big white bow in my hair so that it flopped over the side of my head. Mary Anne couldn't find anything of her own that she really liked, so I loaned her my yellow pedalpushers, a yellow and white striped tank top, and an oversized white jacket. We looked at ourselves in the mirror. Pretty nice! We were ready for a night on the town!

Mary Anne and I went straight to the boardwalk. We ate hamburgers for dinner, which Mary Anne topped off with a couple of pieces of fudge that we had watched being made.

Then we wandered around.

We went to a souvenir stand. Mary Anne bought Sea City visors to bring back to Kristy and Dawn. I bought Claudia a bright yellow T-shirt. It didn't have any words on it, just a hunk surfer. The surfer looked kind of like Scott.

We went to the arcade and played ring toss and penny pitch. We didn't win a thing. I swear those games are rigged.

"Want to ride the Ferris wheel?" Mary Anne asked as we left the arcade.

"Sure," I said.

We sauntered over to a ticket booth. The guy in the booth winked at us.

"Two for the Ferris wheel, please," I said.

"Okay, cutie."

Cutie! In Sea City, there were adorable guys *every*where!

The view from the Ferris wheel was great. When you reached the top, you were pretty high up. Below, lights twinkled in the houses along the beach, the moon cut a path of light across the ocean, and the boardwalk looked like a fairyland.

I don't know quite what made me think of it, but while we were sitting so high up, gazing down at the lights, I suddenly said, "I should buy Scott a present."

"Hmph," was all Mary Anne replied.

Nevertheless, when the Ferris wheel ride was over, I dragged her in and out of store after store. She waited patiently while I chose, then unchose, a book about shells and a blue hat (for when Scott was sitting in the sun); and while I decided for, then against, having a T-shirt printed up that said *Stacey + Scott = LUV*.

We were passing one of the many candy stores on the boardwalk, when suddenly I saw the perfect gift. I ran in and bought it. It cost almost ten dollars, but I didn't care.

Outside the shop I showed Mary Anne the present — a giant red satin heart-shaped box of chocolates.

"This'll really show him how I feel, don't you think, Mary Anne? . . . Mary *Anne?*"

Mary Anne wasn't answering, but she didn't look angry, just preoccupied.

I turned in the direction she was gazing.

"Wait, Stacey," said Mary Anne. "No."

But it was too late. I'd seen.

Snuggled up on a bench behind me were a girl and a guy. The girl was curvy and gorgeous and at least eighteen.

The guy was Scott.

They were kissing.

I turned back to Mary Anne. "Guess I won't be needing this," I said. I thrust the satin box at her. "You take it. You *deserve* it. You were right all along. Enjoy your prize." I burst into tears.

Mary Anne left the unopened box on a bench. Then she put her arm around me and walked me back to the Pikes'.

Sunday night

Dear Dawn,

Stacey is still being a pain, but I feel bad for her because she saw Scott kissing another girl—a much older one—and she started to cry. How is California? I miss you. I'm thinking of getting another bikini at this store here called If the Suit Fits. Stacey got another one. Love,

Mary Anne

P.S. Stacey's been dyeing her hair!
P.P.S. Destroy this card in California!!

As bad as Saturday night was, Sunday morning was just awful. How could I go to the beach and face Scott? I decided there was no way.

After breakfast, I pulled Mrs. Pike and Mary Anne aside. "I have a headache," I said. "Would it be all right if I didn't go to the beach this morning? I'd just like to take it easy. The beach gets so noisy."

"Of course," said Mrs. Pike sympathetically.

"Sure," replied Mary Anne. But up in our room later, she said, "Thanks for sticking me with all the kids again. You know, last night you dragged me around to about a billion stores looking for a present for Scott. Then when you saw him with that girl, you practically blamed *me.* You are so rude. The least you could do is apologize."

"I'm sorry. I really am," I said.

But Mary Anne wasn't finished.

"If you actually had a headache, well, that would be one thing, but it's Scott, isn't it?"

I nodded.

"Boy." Mary Anne shook her head.

"Well, what are you complaining about?" I shot back. What was her problem? I'd already apologized. "That guy mother's helper will be hanging around."

"His name is Alex."

"He looks like such a nerd."

"Well, he's not! He's funny and nice. And he's good with kids."

"Who are those kids, anyway?"

"They're Kenny, Jimmy, and Ellie. Ellie's the baby. And he *is* a mother's helper, but so what? . . . And don't change the subject!"

"What subject?"

"How you've made me do all the work so far."

"I have not."

"Have so."

I sighed. "I'm really sorry, Mary Anne," I said as I followed her downstairs. "I don't know what else to say."

Mary Anne ignored me. She opened the front door. "Come on, kids," she said to the Pikes. "Your mom and dad beat us to the beach this morning."

The Pikes ran outside.

But Byron immediately came back.

"Stacey?" he asked.

"Yeah?"

"Can I stay with you this morning?"

"I guess," I replied, "but I'm not feeling very well. I just want to rest."

"I'll rest, too," he said quietly. He looked awfully serious.

"Okay. Go tell Mary Anne, so she knows where you are."

Byron disappeared. I was kind of glad he wanted to spend the morning with me.

As soon as he came back, he said, "Do you feel like taking a walk? Or are you too sick?"

"No, a walk would be nice," I replied. Then, remembering my "headache," I added, "As long as we go somewhere quiet."

"I know somewhere really quiet," said Byron earnestly. "Come on."

I left a note for Mary Anne and the Pikes. Then Byron led me out the back door, down the street, across the main drag, to the end of the street on the other side of the town.

"This is the bay side of Sea City," Byron informed me.

"Is Sea City on an island?" I asked incredulously.

"Nope, just a little piece of land that curls into the ocean like a dog's tail."

I smiled. "That's a very nice way to describe it," I told Byron.

The bay certainly was quiet. The houses there were even closer to the water than they were on the ocean side, but no one was outdoors. And the water was calm, like a big lake.

Byron waded out to his knees, shaded his

eyes, and said, "See? You can see land across the water. That's the rest of New Jersey."

"Byron!" I exclaimed. "You're in the water!"

Byron looked down. "Oh, yeah," he said. "Hey, here's a little crab or something. . . . Oops, there it goes." The something scuttled away.

"Go after it," I suggested.

Byron shook his head.

"Byron?" I asked. "Are you afraid of the water?"

"Not exactly."

"What do you mean?"

"I don't like the waves. They're too . . . rough. And I don't like it when I can't see the bottom."

So that was why he wouldn't go after the crab. He just didn't want to wade out any farther.

I reached for his hand. "It's really okay, you know," I told him.

Holding my hand, we waded out a few more steps. The water was over our knees.

"Stop!" cried Byron suddenly. "I can't see the bottom. How do you know we're not on the edge of a cliff or something?"

"I don't," I said. "But there's not a good chance of that. Anyway, if we were, and we stepped down, well, we could just turn around and swim to the shore, couldn't we?"

"Yeah. . . ."

"I'll tell you something, Byron. It's smart to be a little afraid of things."

"It is?"

"Yes. Because if you aren't afraid, you might take dangerous chances. But if you're *too* afraid, then you'll probably miss out on a lot of fun."

Byron thought that over. He waded around for a long time, looking for shellfish or for stones to toss. At one point, he said, "Boy, it's hot," and actually ducked under the water briefly.

We walked back to the house shortly after noon. Byron had made me feel as calm as the bay water. I decided I could face the beach. After all, Scott didn't know I'd seen him with the other girl, so it would just be a matter of avoiding him.

While Byron had been thinking and playing, I'd been thinking, too, and I'd figured out what had happened with Scott — or at least I thought I had. I decided that Scott really did like me, but just as a friend. Or maybe even just as a cute kid. He was, as Mary Anne had pointed out, too old for me. The girl I'd seen him with the night before had been much more his age.

She was probably his actual girl friend. I began to feel silly. How could I have thought Scott loved me? He never kissed me, never held my hand, never asked me out. He just sent me off to do favors for him. Still, I couldn't hate him. He'd been nice to me. We'd had fun. He'd given me his whistle.

I was too embarrassed to hang around him anymore, though. Scott might wonder why I was avoiding him. Then again, he might not even notice. Whatever I did probably wouldn't matter, anyway, I thought bitterly. Those other girls would step right back in and take over.

Byron and I returned to the Pikes' in time for lunch. When lunch was over, I whispered to him, "Ready for the beach?"

He nodded, looking scared but determined. Exactly the way I felt.

As it turned out, I didn't need to be scared. Just as we were heading across the sand, the lifeguard jeep pulled up, Scott jumped off the stand, traded places with another guard who'd been in the jeep, and rode away. The next day, I knew, was his day off. I wouldn't have to worry about him until Tuesday. But I couldn't decide whether to feel glad or let down.

Meanwhile, Byron had a terrific afternoon. He waded into the ocean almost up to his knees. While he couldn't be coaxed out any farther, this was good enough for Adam and Jordan. They could do plenty of splashing and shouting in knee-deep water.

I realized how much I'd missed the kids. I'd spent so much time thinking about Scott that I hadn't really been with the Pike kids. Even when I'd been *around* them, I hadn't been *with* them, if you know what I mean. Byron had shown me that.

Mary Anne seemed to be acting a little more friendly. I wasn't sure why, but it might have been the guy mother's helper — Alex, or whatever his name was. The two of them were playing with all eleven of the kids. Whenever I looked at Mary Anne, she was beaming. Her happiness must have canceled out some of her bad feelings about me. I took advantage of her mood to be especially nice to her — and to apologize again.

So, by the end of the day, the triplets were together again, and Mary Anne and I were together again.

But Scott and I had come apart.

Tuesday

Dear Kristy,

Byron went in the water! (Sort of.) I know what he's afaid of. We'll talk about it at the next meeting of the Baby-sitters Club. I heard a really funny joke today. I'll tell that at the next meeting, too.

Luv,
Stacey

Tuesday

Dear Claudia,

I'm IN LUV AGAIN! I met a cute guy named Toby. I mean, really cute. This one is my age, too. He has brown hair, brown eyes, and a few freckles. His clothes are extremely cool.

Luv ya,
Stace

Monday and Tuesday were gorgeous days. I'd been nervous about my decision to avoid Scott, but I didn't need to have been. The very thing that I thought would happen, did happen. All those other girls began hanging around him again, and he called them *cutie* and *beautiful,* just like he'd called me. I have to admit that hurt. I hadn't meant anything to him, after all.

But I stayed with the Pike kids, working hard, and Tuesday passed. Then Wednesday dawned — another clear, sunny morning.

"You know what?" Mary Anne said to me first thing that morning.

"What?" I replied.

"I think some of the kids are getting bored going to the beach every day. Maybe we should split them up. One of us can take the bored ones into town or something, and the other can stay on the beach with the rest of the kids."

"You know, that's a good idea. It's gotten so that Nicky looks a little green every time we mention the beach."

Of course, I was hoping to be the one to go into town, so I could avoid the beach for one more day, but Mary Anne ended up with that job because of her sunburn problem. She took

Nicky, Mallory, Byron, and Margo to Trampoline World and the miniature golf course (Claire had decided she didn't care to use her free passes), and I took Claire, Vanessa, Adam, and Jordan to the beach. (Mr. and Mrs. Pike went to the boardwalk!)

That morning, I had no sooner gotten the kids lathered up with sunscreen, and the chairs and towels set up, than I heard Claire's singsong voice proclaiming that someone was a stupid-silly-billy-goo-goo. I looked around. Not far away were Claire and one of the kids that Mary Anne's friend Alex took care of.

"Stupey-stupey-silly-billy-goo-goo!" Claire sang again. Hands on hips, she faced the little boy.

"Claire Pike!" I shouted, just as the boy burst into tears. I ran over to them. "Claire, what are you doing?"

"Nobody would play with me," she wailed, as if that explained everything. "They're all in the water and they won't play with me."

"So why are you calling this boy a stupey-silly-billy-goo-goo?"

Claire shrugged.

"Well, say you're sorry, and then go lie down on your towel for ten minutes. I'll tell you when the time is up."

"Sorry," mumbled Claire, not sounding as

if she meant it a bit. Then she marched off to our towels.

I looked over at Alex. He and another boy were playing with the baby (Allie? Ellen?) and another little kid on a blanket under an umbrella.

Heaving a deep sigh, I led the crying boy to them.

"Uh-oh," said Alex. "What happened?"

"Claire was teasing him," I explained, pointing to Claire, who was pouting on her towel. "I'm not sure why, but I'm really sorry."

"No problem," replied Alex cheerfully. "Kids are always teasing each other. Listen, you're Stacey, right?" He grinned, and I noticed that he had a very nice smile.

"Right," I said. "And you're Alex."

"Yup. And this is Ellie" — the baby — "Jimmy, Kenny" — who was drying his tears — "and Toby. Toby's my cousin. His family is staying in Sea City for a few days."

That was when I got my first really good look at Toby. He was about fourteen years old. (Perfect!) His brown hair was sort of waved back from his face. It was held out of his eyes with a blue headband. I was glad I could see his eyes, because they were a beautiful deep brown, almost velvety looking. A handful of freckles was sprinkled across his nose and cheeks. He was wearing plain white swimming trunks, but his shirt was amazing — tan with silly pictures of cowboy boots and cactuses all over it. And his sunglasses — black bands with narrow slits from side to side to see through. Totally cool. I wished Claudia had been there.

"Hi," I said, hoping I didn't sound too eager.

"Hi," he replied, sounding as eager as I had tried not to sound.

There was an awkward pause.

"Well," I said, "I better get back to Claire."

"Okay."

Disappointed, I wandered back to our stuff. But when Claire's ten minutes were up and the two of us began to amble toward the ocean, Toby ran after us. "Hey," he said to Claire, "do you know how to make witches' castles?"

Claire looked intrigued. "No," she replied. "How?"

Toby led us to a patch of wet sand just beyond where the waves were coming in. (I noticed, thankfully, that we were yards down the beach from the lifeguard stand.) He showed Claire how to drip the wet sand through her fingers to make weird, blobby fairy-taleish shapes.

Soon Claire was making a whole row of castles. She left Toby and me behind.

"Well," I said after a while, "where do you live?"

"Lawrenceville, New Jersey," replied Toby. "How about you?"

"Stoneybrook, Connecticut. But I grew up in New York."

"New York *City?*"

"Yeah."

"Wow."

Toby was fourteen. He was going to be a freshman in high school. He played soccer and football. His hobby was computers. He had two older sisters. His favorite group was Smash. His favorite food was peanut butter. He hated history and geography. He liked math. He loved telling jokes. He didn't look at a single girl except me while we were talking.

By the end of the morning, he and I knew everything about each other. And the two of us and Claire, joined by Alex, his kids, and Adam, Jordan, and Vanessa, had built an entire village of castles. People walking along the beach would pause to watch us.

We hated to stop for lunch, but we had to. We were all dying of starvation. Afterward, though, we came right back. The waves had destroyed part of our village, but we started building again, anyway.

"So," said Toby, as he topped off a large castle, "did you hear about the dying man named Al who wanted a city named after him?"

"No," I replied, smiling.

"Well, this guy Al knows he hasn't got much time left, so he says to his friend, 'Promise me they'll name a city after me.' And his friend says, 'I promise, Al.' And Al says, 'Will it be big?' and the friend says, 'Sure will, Al,' and Al says, 'Will it be pretty?' and the friend says, 'Count on it, Al.' "

"They named a city Al?" I interrupted.

Toby grinned and went right on. "And Al says, 'And you *promise* it'll be named after me?' and the friend says, 'You betcha, Mr. Buquerque.' Get it?" said Toby. "The guy's name was Al Buquerque? *Al*buquerque? As in New Mexico?"

"I get it," I said. I fell over in the sand, laughing hysterically.

Claire pounced on me. "Stacey-silly-billy-goo-goo!"

And Vanessa commented, "Joking, playing in the sun. Now this is what's called lots of fun!"

I looked up at Toby. He looked down at me.

We began to laugh.

I was in love again.

Friday

Dear Kristy,

The kids are antsy. It's their last day here. They want to do everything "one last time." But they're also excited about coming home. I'll probably see you before you get this card!

Luv,
Stacey

Friday

Dear Claudia,

I'm going out with Toby tonight. For real! We have an evening on the boardwalk planned. I'll tell you all about it when I see you.

Luv ya!
Stace

Friday was our last day in Sea City. The next morning, we would pack up the car and leave. I couldn't believe the two weeks were almost over.

Guess how Mrs. Pike began our last day. She said to Mary Anne and me, "You girls deserve another night off. At five o'clock this afternoon you're on your own. Just be home by ten."

We were ecstatic! But we tried not to show just how ecstatic we were. We didn't want the kids to think we didn't enjoy taking care of them.

Friday's weather was not the greatest. It was in and out, cloudy and sunny. And rain was predicted for the next day. I thought that was a good thing, because going home would be easier if we weren't leaving brilliant sunshine behind.

However, despite the clouds, the kids wanted to go to the beach. "I wanna make one last witch castle," said Claire.

"We wanna play one last game of shark," said Jordan.

Each kid had a last "wanna." While they were taking care of the wannas, I said to Mary Anne, "I just had a great idea! What if Alex could get tonight off, too? Maybe you and I and Alex and Toby could go to the boardwalk together or something."

"Together?" repeated Mary Anne warily.

"You know," I said. "A sort of, um, double date."

Mary Anne turned pale.

"Mary Anne, I said *double* date, not *blind* date. It's not as if you've never seen Alex before. You know him. You like him."

"But girls aren't supposed to ask guys out."

"Oh, Mary Anne, that is so old-fashioned. Besides, this is our last chance. If we don't say something, and we don't go out with Toby and Alex tonight, we'll probably never see them again."

"That's true. . . ."

"Good. Now go ask Alex if he can get the night off."

"*Me?!* This was your idea."

"Yeah, but Alex is your friend," I told her.

Well, Mary Anne surprised me. She got up and walked over to Alex's spot on the beach. I watched her in her caftan and baseball cap. I wished I could hear what she was saying, but the wind was blowing in the wrong direction. All I know is that she came back with a grin on her face, looking a little smug, actually, and said, "We're on. We're supposed to meet them at Hercules' Hot Dogs at six o'clock."

* * *

Mary Anne and I spent almost an hour — from five until quarter to six — getting ready to see Toby and Alex. We didn't have much choice about what to wear, so we ended up in the same clothes we'd worn on our last night off, but we kept thinking of other things to do.

"I better file my nails," said Mary Anne. "They're all ragged."

"I better put on nail polish," I replied. "I've got pink sparkles and yellow sparkles. Want to borrow the yellow?"

"Sure! Oh, and I should put on hand lotion."

"My perfume!" I cried. "Where is it?"

"I don't know. Do you have any lip gloss?"

"Sure. Here. . . . Ew! Look at my hair."

"Yours! Ew! Look at mine!"

Somehow, though, we were on our way to the boardwalk at 5:45, and standing in front of Hercules' at 5:55. The boys showed up promptly at six.

Mary Anne elbowed me when she saw them heading toward us. "Doesn't Alex look great?" she whispered excitedly.

He did look great, but I thought Toby looked greater. (I didn't say so, of course.) Toby was wearing these baggy white cotton pants and an oversized blue and white striped sweater. Totally cool.

"Hey," he said, taking me by the elbow.

"Hi," I replied. "I'm glad you could come tonight."

"Me, too."

"Are you guys hungry?" I asked.

"Starved," said Alex. "Let's eat."

Hercules' main feature was hot dogs that really were an entire foot long. We sat at the counter and gave our orders to a waitress. (I got a hamburger.) Mary Anne and I ate about two thirds of our food. The boys finished their hot dogs. Then they finished our food. Then they each ordered another dog. Mary Anne began to look a little green just watching them eat. They kept slathering the dogs up with mustard, and dumping spoonfuls of sauerkraut on them, while Toby told the longest joke in the history of comedy.

In order to get Mary Anne's eyes off the hot dogs, I nudged her and murmured, "Mary Anne?"

"Yeah?" she whispered.

"Would it be okay with you if Toby and I went off by ourselves for a while? I mean, would you feel okay about being alone with Alex?"

Mary Anne looked thoughtful. Then a slow smile spread across her face. "Yeah," she said. "I *would* feel okay!"

I grinned. If we hadn't been sitting in the middle of Hercules' Hot Dogs, I would have hugged her.

At last, the ends of the boys' hot dogs disappeared into their mouths. We left Hercules'.

"What do you want to do now?" asked Alex.

"Look around the stores," Mary Anne replied.

"Go to the arcade," I replied.

So we split up.

Toby and I played a dart-throwing game. I won a hat for him. He won a teddy bear for me. (Later I named the bear Toby-Bear.) It must have been beginner's luck (or maybe beginner's *love*) because after that we played three other games and didn't win anything.

It was starting to grow dark. "Let's walk around," I said. I liked just looking at the lights and listening to the boardwalk sounds and smelling the boardwalk smells.

We came to a shell shop and peered in. "Come on," said Toby.

Inside were shelves and bins full of nothing but seashells. I was pouring through a box of tiny conch shells when Toby handed me a little paper bag.

"What's this?" I asked as we walked outside.

"Open it."

I did. Inside was a shiny pale pink shell.

"It's to remember me by," said Toby.

For some reason, I couldn't smile at him. I felt like crying, instead. "Thanks," I whispered.

Toby took my hand. "Hey, there's the Tunnel of Luv! Let's buy tickets for it!"

The Tunnel of Luv was like no ride I'd ever been on. It wasn't noisy, it didn't jerk you around corners, and nothing jumped out at you. Toby and I sat side by side in this boat shaped like a swan and floated lazily through a dark tunnel in which soft music was playing.

Just before we left the tunnel, Toby leaned over and kissed me gently.

My first kiss! I couldn't believe it!

I knew I would never forget Sea City or the boardwalk or the Tunnel of Luv.

Or Toby.

I would never, *ever* forget Toby.

I didn't want Saturday morning to come. I wanted Friday night in Sea City to last forever. Toby and me in the Tunnel of Luv.

But there was no stopping Saturday. I woke up early that morning and lay in bed, just thinking and remembering. I looked over at Mary Anne, who was curled up in a ball. Her hair was falling across her face and she was breathing deeply.

Outside the window, the waves crashed, pounding the shore. The sky was a threatening gray. A lone sea gull wheeled low over the sand. The salt air came in our open window on a breeze that felt chilly. I pulled my covers more tightly around me. It seemed like the end of summer as well as the end of our vacation.

I was amazed at all the things that had happened in the last two weeks. I'd been away from home. I'd stayed on my diet and taken my insulin and hadn't gotten sick. I'd met two boys I liked, and one of them had kissed me.

I smiled.

Toby was going to come by that morning to say good-bye. I was excited and sad at the same time.

"Stacey-silly-billy-goo-goo?" whispered a voice.

I tiptoed to the door and opened it. There stood Claire. She was stark naked.

"Claire! What are you doing?"

"Looking for my bathing suit," she replied. "Will you come to the beach with me?"

"Sure," I said. An early morning walk might be nice. "But it's too cold for a suit. Why don't you get dressed very quietly? I'll meet you downstairs in a few minutes."

When Claire and I were dressed, we put on sweat shirts and tiptoed out the front door of the Pikes' house. The sky and the ocean were almost the same color — flat gray — but no rain was falling.

Claire ran to the water's edge.

"Don't go in!" I called after her.

"I won't," she said. "I'm just looking."

Claire stood and looked forever. I'd never seen her stay in one place for so long. While she was looking, I stooped down and picked up a piece of driftwood. Then I found a flat patch of wet sand and wrote

STACEY + TOBY = LUV

I watched and watched, but the waves didn't wash it away.

At breakfast that morning, Mr. Pike finished his eggs, wiped his mouth, and said, "Hey, hey, everybody! Guess what it's time for?"

"What, Daggles-silly-billy-goo-goo?" asked Claire, bouncing around in her chair.

"The . . . chore-hat!"

"Oh, no. Oh, no," moaned Mallory.

The triplets groaned.

Mary Anne and I looked at each other and shrugged.

"I've put the names of eight chores in the hat," Mr. Pike went on. "Pass it around, kids. We have work to do this morning. And we have to leave by one o'clock."

Reluctantly, the Pike kids passed the hat. Each ended up with a chore such as sweeping the porch or collecting the sand pails. I realized we had a lot to do before we left for Stoneybrook.

"Stacey and Mary Anne," said Mrs. Pike, "can you supervise the children's packing?"

"Sure," we replied.

A couple of hours later, the kids had finished their chores, and were fairly well packed-up. Mr. and Mrs. Pike were working away, but they turned us loose on the beach. Although the day was still gray, the air was warmer and it hadn't rained yet. The lifeguards were on duty, so the kids ran to the water for a final swim.

Mary Anne and I sat down on our towels. (We hadn't brought anything else to the beach.)

"It's almost over," said Mary Anne sadly.

"It seems like we just got here," I told her.

"Yeah."

We hugged our knees and looked out at the ocean. Scott was on the guard station, but I barely noticed him. I was thinking of Toby.

Mary Anne looked dreamy-eyed. She'd already told me what she and Alex had done the night before. They'd sat by the ocean and talked, and then they'd gone through the Tunnel of Luv, too.

"Hey," she said. "Look who's coming."

Toby and Alex were heading across the sand with Kenny, Jimmy, and Ellie.

We waved to them. "Come sit over here," I called.

The boys came over, but they didn't sit down. "We're just out for a walk," said Alex.

"We have to get back, but we wanted to say good-bye."

"Oh, no!" cried Mary Anne. "I hate good-byes."

They had to be said, though, because the boys really couldn't stay.

Toby walked me away from the others so we could have a little privacy.

"Promise you'll write?" I said. We had exchanged addresses the night before.

"I promise. Do you?"

I nodded. I'm not much of a letter-writer, but maybe I'd feel different about writing to Toby.

"Well . . ." said Toby.

"Well . . ." I said.

"I guess this is it."

"Yeah, I guess. . . ."

"I want to kiss you," Toby whispered, "but there are too many people around."

"That's okay," I said. (The sixteen eyes of the Pike kids were boring holes into us, all the way from the ocean.)

"Will you remember me?" asked Toby.

"Always. By the shell and by the bear."

"I'll remember you by the hat." Toby was wearing it. He patted it fondly.

"Well," said Toby again. "'Bye, Stacey."

"'Bye," I replied.

I stayed where I was and watched him walk back to Alex and the kids. A few moments later, they started up the beach, leaving Mary Anne by herself. Toby turned around once to wave to me. Then they disappeared behind a sand dune.

I ran to Mary Anne. She was crying.

"Mary Anne!" I whispered. "All the kids are watching."

"I know, I know." She wiped her eyes. "I'm really okay."

I gave her a quick hug. "We'll talk about this at home tonight, okay?"

Mary Anne nodded.

My eyes drifted across the beach to the lifeguard stand — and Scott. For some reason, he turned around then. He saw me and waved.

I waved back. "Mary Anne," I said, "there's something I have to do. It'll only take a minute."

I ran across the sand to Scott.

"Hey, babe," he greeted me. "Long time no see."

"I've been busy," I replied vaguely. "We're leaving today."

"You are? Hey, too bad, love. I'll miss you."

What he'll miss, I thought, is someone to run errands for him. But somehow I couldn't feel mad about that anymore, because I knew

Scott really did like me, even if he didn't love me.

"Thanks again for your whistle," I said. "I'll always keep it." I'd never wear it, but I'd keep it to remind me of the first boy I ever fell in love with. I'd put it in a drawer, though. Not on a shelf, where I planned to sit Toby-Bear, or on my dresser, where I planned to put the seashell.

"Hey, Stacey!" Byron yelled to me from the water's edge. "Mom's calling us!"

I turned around. Mrs. Pike was at the front door of the house, signaling to us. The rest of the Pike kids were wading ashore. Mary Anne was gathering up towels.

"I have to go," I said. "I hope you like college, Scott."

"Thanks. You be good now, babe."

I joined the Pike kids and herded them across the sand to Mary Anne. Just as we were running into the house, rain began to fall.

Claire burst into tears. "I don't want to leave!" she cried.

I picked her up and gave her a hug. "I don't want to either, but it's time to leave. Hey, you'll be coming back next summer. Think of that."

"Yeah," said Claire, sniffling. "And we can eat at Gurber Garden."

"And play miniature golf."

"And jump on the trapperleens." Claire began to smile.

When everyone was dressed, we loaded up the cars. We seemed to have an awful lot more stuff than we'd left Stoneybrook with. But after pushing and shoving and groaning, we found places for everything and everyone.

We split into the same traveling groups as before.

As we were pulling out of the driveway, Mr. Pike called to Mrs. Pike, "First stop, Ellen Cooke's to return the keys. Next stop, Howard Johnson's."

"Jingle bells, Santa smells," sang Nicky.

"I *hate* that song, Nicholas," said Mallory.

"Good-bye, Sea City-silly-billy-goo-goo!" cried Claire.

"Where's the Barf Bucket?" asked Margo.

I sighed. We were on our way home.

"Hi, Mom! Hi, Dad! I'm home!"

I let myself into our house, feeling absolutely exhausted. Claire had asked, "How many more minutes till we get there?" twenty-nine times between Howard Johnson's and Stoneybrook.

"Stacey!" My parents ran out of the kitchen and folded me into a happy three-person hug.

"How are you?" asked Dad.

"Did you have fun?" asked Mom.

"What did you do?" asked Dad.

"Did you take your insulin every day?" asked Mom.

"Look at your tan!" exclaimed Dad.

"What happened to your hair?" asked Mom.

Although we had left rain behind in Sea City, the sun was shining in Stoneybrook. Mom and Dad and I sat out on our back deck and talked and talked. I didn't exactly tell my parents everything (I left out Scott and Toby), but I told them a lot. I told them how easy it had been to stick to my diet, and that I never once forgot my insulin. That was the truth. And I told them that the sun had lightened my hair. That was half the truth.

"What's gone on around here?" I wanted to know.

"It's been pretty quiet," said Mom. "Oh, before I forget, Claudia phoned about an hour ago. The Kishis are back, and she wants you to call her."

"Okay," I said, but I was in no hurry to move. I was too tired. Dad made iced tea and we sat on the deck and drank it as the sun dropped behind the trees in the yard.

I waited until after dinner before I went to my room and picked up the phone. I wished I had my own private telephone number like Claudia did, but I knew I was lucky even to have an extension in my room. I closed my door. Then I lay down on my bed.

I dialed Mary Anne. I was dying to call Claudia, but I knew Mary Anne needed me, and I really wanted to talk to her.

"Hi," I said when she answered. "It's me, Stacey. I wanted to see how you're doing."

"Oh, I'm fine," said Mary Anne. "I'm sorry I cried before. I just didn't think saying good-bye to him — Alex, I mean — would be so sad. I didn't — Oh, I don't know. I'm so embarrassed."

"Don't be embarrassed. Why are you embarrassed?"

"I don't know."

"Mary Anne, he's a *boy*," I told her. "And it's okay to like a boy."

"But I never liked one before. I've always been sort of afraid of them."

"Then I'm glad you met Alex. I'm glad he helped change your mind about boys. They're not alien creatures, you know."

Mary Anne giggled. "I know. Hey, Stace? I want to tell you something. I understand now how you felt about Scott at first. I'm sorry I gave you such a hard time about not helping out and everything."

"That's okay. I guess I really wasn't being very fair. I did stick you with more than your share of the work. And that wasn't right. Besides, when a person is baby-sitting, the kids should come first, no matter what. Do you forgive me?"

"Sure," replied Mary Anne. "Do you forgive me?"

"Of course."

"Hey," said Mary Anne, starting to giggle.

"Remember when all the Pike kids tried to give me sunburn remedies?"

"Yeah. And when Claire won those free games from Fred?"

"And the look on Adam's face when Nicky got the hole in one?"

"And the look on *your* face when Alex said he and Toby would double-date with us?!"

We were laughing hysterically.

"I wonder if anyone ever found the box of chocolates you left on the bench on the boardwalk?" I went on. Thinking about Scott and the girl made me sad, but I could remember the chocolates and laugh, or look at his whistle and smile.

"Oh, I hope so," said Mary Anne. "Listen to me. I'm laughing so hard I'm crying." I could hear her sniffling and snuffling.

"Did you and Alex exchange addresses?" I asked.

"Yup." There was a pause. "We exchanged something else, too," she said finally.

"What?!"

"On the boardwalk, on Friday night. I didn't exactly tell you the whole story."

"Yeah?"

"We found this place where you can buy rings and have stuff engraved on them. They were only five dollars each. So he has a ring with my initials, and I have one with his."

"Ooh, Mary Anne, a ring!" I exclaimed. "That sounds serious."

"Well, it isn't," she replied. "I mean, not really."

"Are you going to wear it?"

"On a chain around my neck, not on my finger. I don't want Dad to see it. He'd probably lock me up until I'm twenty-one."

"Maybe not," I said.

"Maybe not," she agreed.

"Listen, I have to go," I told Mary Anne. "Claudia called this afternoon, and I haven't called her back yet."

"Okay. I guess I should call Dawn and Kristy."

"Mary Anne?"

"Yeah?"

"I'm really glad we got to know each other better."

"Oh, me, too!"

"Well, 'bye."

"'Bye."

I pressed the button, listened for the dial tone, and called Claudia without even hanging up the phone.

She answered on the first ring. "Aughh! Hi! I can't believe I'm talking to you! How come it took so long for you to call? How are you? How was the trip? Oh, I got all your postcards! I'm really sorry about Scott."

I laughed. "How are *you?*"

"Great. Our vacation was fabulous! It was good for Mimi. She's getting better. And there were arts and crafts at the place we went to, and I threw a pot."

"You *what?*"

"I threw a pot."

"Why?"

"I mean, I *made* a pot — you know, on a potter's wheel. That's what it's called. Throwing a pot."

"Oh."

"The teacher said it was the best one she'd ever seen a beginner make. So Mom and Dad said maybe I could take a pottery class here when school begins."

"That's great. . . . Did you meet anyone interesting?"

"You mean, any interesting guys?"

"Of course."

"Of course."

"You did?"

"Yeah. His name is Skip. He's three. I baby-sat for him."

"No, seriously!" I cried.

"Seriously," said Claudia, "there weren't

any guys my age up there. Unfortunately. But I was busy enough just reading your postcards. So what finally happened with Scott and Toby? And what was the great present Scott gave you?"

"Oh, Scott gave me his lifeguard whistle. I'll show it to you sometime. And he and I are friends, although we'll probably never see each other again, or even write. And Toby and I are, well. . . ."

"What?!"

"On our last night in Sea City, Mrs. Pike gave Mary Anne and me the evening off, and we went on a double date with Toby and his cousin Alex."

I could almost hear Claudia's jaw drop. "Mary Anne went out on a double *date?*"

"Yup."

"With a *boy?*"

"What else?"

"I can't believe it. I can't believe it."

"And she really likes the guy," I added. "Anyway, after we ate supper, we split up, and Toby bought me a pink seashell to remember him by. He won a teddy bear for me, too. We're going to write each other. I hope."

"He sounds really nice, Stace," said Claudia.

"Yeah. . . ."

"How are the Pike kids?"

"Oh, they're fine. I think they had a great time. I feel like I know them so well now — I mean, *understand* them. You know why Nicky's a pest?"

"Why?"

"Because he wants to be 'one of the guys,' but sometimes the triplets don't let him play with them. Then he feels left out of the whole family. And Byron's different than we thought he was. He's quieter than Adam and Jordan, more serious. Kind of sensitive. And Vanessa can drive you crazy with this poetry kick she's on, but she's really a good little kid. Oh, and Mallory was a *big* help. We put her in charge of a few of the kids sometimes, and she did fine. Listen, when are we having our next Baby-sitters Club meeting? Monday?"

"I think so. We're all back."

"Great. I can't wait to talk to Dawn and see how California was. And Kristy must have had a trillion sitting jobs while we were all away."

"There's only one bad thing about all this," said Claudia.

"What?"

"The summer's almost over. School's going to begin again."

"Yeah," I replied, "but not for two weeks. And you don't know *what* could happen in two weeks. Almost anything. After all, in two weeks I found my first real love, lost him, found another, and got my first kiss."

"Your first *kiss!* You didn't say anything about that!"

"Oh . . . didn't I?" I replied casually.

"No! Tell me."

"Okay."

I knew we'd be on the phone for at least an hour, but who cared? After all, I was in love.

Form Your Own

You and your friends can form your own chapter of The Baby-Sitters Club with your official Baby-Sitters Club Kit! Here's how:

1. Write down your favorite baby-sitting tip. How do you make your job easier? Handle emergencies? Quiet crying babies? Get kids to go to bed on time? **OR...**

Tell us about your funniest baby-sitting experience. The weirdest family you ever sat for...the scariest thing that ever happened while you were sitting...the strangest kid...the most ridiculous "baby-sitting disaster!"

2. Send us your tip or story, plus $1.95 to cover shipping and handling. We'll send you a Membership Charter, Parent Emergency Info Sheets, and more...PLUS, we'll choose the best tips and stories for The Baby-Sitters Club Newsletter, also included!

Send check or money order (no cash please), and your tip or story (write your name, address and age on each page) to:

The Baby-Sitters Club
Scholastic Books
Promotion Dept., 10th floor
730 Broadway
New York, NY 10003

Offer good while supply lasts.

BSC871